It's Always Darkest Before the Dawn

Cordy Jiang

DEDICATION

To my mom Leslie, my dad William, and my brother Cosmo for guiding me to the dawn.

Copyright © 2018 Cordy Jiang

All rights reserved.

ISBN: 978-1-9809-3499-8

CONTENTS

	Acknowledgments	i
1	The Robot She Built	1
2	The Music of the Forest	9
3	Casper	16
4	After Isabel	22
5	Mommy	28
6	The Silver Rings	33
7	Professor Washington	37
8	The Colors of Our Souls	44
9	In Her Dreams	51
10	It's Always Darkest Before the Dawn	54
11	The Therapist I Fell in Love With	60
12	Bombay Oven	67
	Additional Poems	72

ACKNOWLEDGMENTS

This collection would not be possible without the support of the students and faculty in UCSC's Creative Writing Program. A special thanks to Professor Melissa Sanders-Self and Professor Karen Tei Yamashita for their encouragement and guidance.

1 THE ROBOT SHE BUILT

Stop it! Please stop. God, no not this again. I can't stand it. It's all happening, and I'm watching it unfold. I'm watching people die, knowing I can save them and consciously choosing not to. Imagine that. Imagine being forced to watch someone repeat your worst mistakes right in front of you. Imagine knowing the secret to life and not being able to share that miracle of truth with those who need it the most. Does that make me a passive murderer? Maybe it does. Am I selfish to not share my knowledge with those whose livelihood depend on it? Maybe I am. But you know what? I've worked hard to earn it, so I'm free to do with it what I want. I remember when I was convinced I'd never be over it, but I am now…I have to be. So, why don't we drop the subject? I'll back it up a few years and tell you the story of two lovebirds instead.

Once upon a time, in a university far, far away, there was a girl named Lara. She was the epitome of a siren and the most skilled man-eater around, strutting about campus in her high heel shoes and designer clothes. She went about her days confidently and carelessly thinking that she was what everyone dreamed of having. Lara thought herself to be by far the best catch around. Little did she know, most people saw right through her ruse; to most people, she was nothing but narcissistic and inconsiderate trash. However, these people learned to hold their tongues to spare themselves the drama; instead, they sat by idly while a naïve few couldn't see past Lara's disguise and as a result, went into a hypnotic trance around her.

One man's trash is another man's treasure, and there were plenty of boys who were blinded by her beauty. It was always the nice and wholesome boys who would fall into her trap and be cast under her spell. Lara herself had grown accustomed to this and assumed everyone wanted her the way these naive few did. However, when it was brought to her attention that she had ensnared a girl, she felt genuinely tempted. How exciting would that be! Lara sat there fantasizing about how wild it would be to rebel against her religious morals and fall into lust with a girl. The more she entertained this idea, the stronger her desire would grow. After all, college was an ideal time and place for sexual experimentation, and Lara's parents weren't around to supervise and control her every action now. While embarking on this chapter of undergraduate college life, Lara began flirting back to her classmate and floormate: Sasha. Sasha always made subtle advances, being quite the inexperienced one but too embarrassed to admit her inexperience. On many levels, Sasha was too good for Lara, and all of their mutual friends would attest to that. Sasha was incredibly special, sensitive, and vibrant; however, Lara never learned to see her this way – the way Sasha deserved to be seen, the way most people saw her. It's sad the people we love the most in this world think that we hate them the most and that the people we hate the most in this world think that we love them the most. The world will forever lose people to this idea until we all wake up and smell the coffee.

Despite being polar opposites, Lara and Sasha both wanted something more than friendship, but they had very different views on romance, and a relationship meant drastically different things to both girls.

Sasha thought she could only get whatever other people wanted to give and as a result, wasn't good at drawing boundaries with people. The combination of these led her to be taken advantage of time after time. Her inaccurate perspective of herself stemmed from her low self-esteem and was one of many symptoms of her insecurity.

Sasha was always so invested in the people around her, and she made it her priority to keep track of everyone else and tend to their needs the way a best friend would, but it's tiring being everyone's best friend. She wanted everyone to be happy and somehow always knew how to make that possible. Needless to say, Sasha was caring and thoughtful, but these were also her biggest flaws. She was everyone's busy little bumblebee, and the more people she knew, the busier she would get. Her consideration of others was always what got her in trouble, because she simply cared too much and didn't know her limits. Her limits already far exceeded those of others, yet she would still keep pushing. This did not go unnoticed. Pretty, attentive, and loyal, Sasha was thought of highly and loved by many. Naturally, everyone worried about Sasha and felt protective of her, so imagine their dismay when Lara slowly began sucking her soul away.

Sasha went to school everyday concerned for her classmates rather than the class material. Academics always took a backseat to her family and friends, so imagine her family's outrage when they started seeing Lara and Sasha together. Lara was clearly and recklessly corrupting and tainting their precious gem.

With Sasha and Lara living on the same floor of the same dorm building and majoring in the same department, their friendship was inevitable... but they went the extra step in unfolding a romance. It started when Lara's birthday was coming up, and it seemed like all anyone could talk about. Lara was polarizing; people either loved her or hated her. Thus, her birthday was not to be forgotten. Now that Sasha was in Lara's life, both of their friend groups doubled, and everyone began paying both of them much more attention. Being the generous and giving person Sasha was, she frequented the local favorite restaurant – Moosewood - and picked up a $100 dollar gift card for her new best friend, Lara. Lara eagerly snatched up the gift card like a green-eyed monster. Sasha had been saving up for a while for this gift, because she wanted to make her first move a memorable one.

Sasha vividly remembered the experience she had buying the gift card at Moosewood. She had just deposited her last paycheck on her way there. As Sasha stood in line at the host stand, she anxiously tapped her foot and dealt with racing thoughts and insecurities about how much to put on the card. She wanted Lara to know that she cared, but not that she cared too much...just more than a regular friend would.

"Wow you guys are busy today. I guess you always are. Umm, I'm sorry to bother you, but I was wondering if you guys sell gift cards? I'm looking to buy one for a good friend," Sasha asked as she reached the host stand.

Sasha overzealously reasoned that $100 was the rule of thumb for gifts given amongst their age range, which was definitely on the generous side considering they had only known each other a few weeks; it was only the first month of their freshman year at school. Sasha was always giving and in this case, more than willing to dish out the money. Sasha experienced the most pleasure when pleasuring others, and she knew from inside sources that Lara absolutely loved this restaurant. As Sasha handed over her hard-earned $100 bill in return for a gift card, all that was on her mind were fantasies of Lara and her going on a romantic candlelit dinner there.

Little did she know, their future would hold so much more in store for them and that Lara's affection could be bought by money. For Sasha, money was a natural gesture appropriate for special occasions, but she would soon find out money was in fact the center of Lara's world and that Lara's love language translated into a plethora of expensive gifts.

When Sasha finally returned to the dorms after venturing off campus to go to the restaurant, she nervously strolled to Lara's door, ready to deliver the card. When Sasha reached Lara's door, she took a few deep breaths and knocked on Lara's door with false confidence. No reply. That's odd, Sasha thought to herself, I can swear I hear voices inside. So, Sasha waited a few moments before knocking again.

"Oh hey! What's up girl?" A disheveled and underdressed Lara answered the door breathlessly.

"Hi! Nothing!" Sasha nervously replied, "I suppose I just wanted to drop off this birthday card for you."

In the background, Sasha heard someone ruffling in Lara's bed sheets but pretended to hear nothing. She handed over the card, flashed a fake smile, and hastily bid Lara goodbye. Lara stood there in the doorway, eagerly opening the birthday card, snatching the gift card inside of it, and briskly putting it away in her wallet the way a bank teller processes money. Lara was so impressed with the amount of money that she knew she not only wanted more but that she could also get more. Sasha would soon be her new source of money. Thus, Lara put in the effort of writing a red, heart-shaped note and slipping it under Sasha's door. She didn't bother to knock on Sasha's door and hand it to her in person, because frankly, she didn't care.

Later that day, as Sasha discovered and hastily read this enticing note, she felt her pull towards Lara come more to life. She wasn't sure exactly what it was that was so alluring about Lara, but a passionate and instinctual excitement began to stir within Sasha's gut. Her life had changed, and the process was irreversible. It was like Lara had somehow cast a spell on her, and Sasha was feeling its full effect. Why the hell not? Sasha thought to herself. After all, from the little Sasha knew of Lara, she smelled good, looked good, and felt good. Most of all, Sasha had finally found someone that received her gifts as much as she wished to give them. Clearly, the relationship was a one-way street from the start, but no one dared point out that obvious truth to Sasha; it was as if they all abided by the same social contract - they believed in the practice of learning from one's own mistakes and keeping silent even in moments of outrage. The pair began spending every hour together, whether in or out of a classroom setting and whether school was on break or not. They would go to the gym together, eat at the dining halls together, study at the library together, team up for school projects together, attend professors' office hours together, walk to class together, experiment with drugs together, travel to nearby cities together, and even attend concerts and raves together over breaks from school. Now, if this all seems overwhelming and stimulating for your senses...that's because it was. The girls became kindred spirits, and there was no way Lara would lift her spell as she began observing more and more perks out of the relationship. Sasha could do her homework for them, plan fun excursions for them, and please Lara physically. Sasha made this relationship her paramount priority, but Lara could care less. Lara was apathetic about the whole relationship, knowing full well how wrapped around her finger Sasha was. In fact, the harder Sasha tried, the less Lara cared, because Lara was certain she possessed Sasha completely.

Lara loved Sasha the only way she knew how to love someone – selfishly. Her warped view on love meant accepting financial and sexual favors in a very cold, technical, and heartless way. Lara continued keeping all of her friends close, while Sasha sacrificed the relationships she had with her closest loved ones in order to devote more time and effort to Lara. At times, the clouds of denial that blinded Sasha would temporarily clear up, and she would cry herself to sleep, thinking about how miserable her life had become. This unrequited love was tearing her apart. However, every time Lara felt Sasha slipping through her fingers, all she had to do was whisper a few sweet nothings into Sasha's ear, and the spell would be cast all over again.

Completely taking advantage of her power, Lara began wrongly creating and enforcing unhealthy new rules for their relationship and constantly pushed boundaries to inappropriate levels – whether mental or physical. Sasha kept letting it slide, thinking these compromises must be normal in all relationships, and that this was simply her first time being in a relationship, so of course there would be a few hiccups here and there. However, Sasha's abnormally high pain tolerance meant that a lot of Lara's tricks were beyond inappropriate yet still acceptable by Sasha's standards. For all Sasha naively knew, everyone was pure at heart and always had good intentions, but unfortunately, that was far from the truth in Lara's case.

Sasha made the fatal mistake of thinking that this increasingly abusive relationship with Lara was that one true love that she had always dreamed and fantasized about. In Sasha's defense, this is one of the most common mistakes of all mankind. The trap of the Stockholm Syndrome is no joke; in fact, it's a slippery, slippery slope. As Sasha's captor, Lara was only eating away at Sasha's soul an undetectable a bite a day, allowing just enough time and space for Sasha's naïve denial to cover up Lara's wrongs. Before she knew it, Sasha had begun running all of Lara's errands, getting street drugs for Lara, making fake ID's for Lara, ditching class to for Lara, etc. Sasha had become a robot – a robot running on the batteries of obsession. Naturally, Sasha's loved ones saw less and less of her, because it was more painful for them to see her in her current state than to not see her at all. And so it was, Sasha's bridges began burning one at a time, slowly but surely.

As freshmen year ended, the two said their goodbyes before summer vacation, though of course they made plans to see each other over the next few months. Upon parting, Sasha gave Lara a promise ring that she hoped would symbolize a lifetime's worth of love and affection. The first thing Lara did was inspect the ring until she found the inscription confirming it was real sterling silver, and only then did she offer an unexcited response .

"Thanks, I guess," Lara mumbled.

The truth was, at that point, Lara loved the sterling silver ring more than she loved Sasha.

Over summer vacation, Sasha kept in close touch with Lara until finally it escalated to the point where Sasha booked a flight to Lara's hometown. Of course, in preparation for their time spent together, Sasha smuggled ecstasy, cocaine, and weed onto the plane with her to see Lara, understanding that doing drugs had become a common activity for the two of them and the only way Lara could have a good time anymore. If Sasha were anything, it was stubborn and daring. She was stubborn about her love for Lara and daring in the risks she would take for her. Fortunately, notorious TSA dogs were nowhere to be found. The risk of being caught was nowhere near what Sasha was willing to risk for Lara; Sasha's addiction to Lara was far stronger than her addiction to any of the substances. As for Lara, she sure did love her free drugs. Sasha stopped bothering to ask Lara to chip in for things like this, knowing that it became expected of her to provide all the entertainment.

Being the cautious and considerate partner Sasha was, she would spend careful amounts of time experimenting with any new hard drug on her own before deeming it safe or fun enough for her Lara. Thus, Lara's first time rolling on ecstasy would be during this beautiful summer on the beaches of her hometown. Sasha had it all ready: the pacifiers, the Vick's VapoInhalers, the bandanas, the perfect music playlists, etc. Lara loved it.

The pattern of their relationship was a rollercoaster for Sasha and a tricycle ride for Lara. The dynamics were completely and fatally unbalanced. When it came to sex, Sasha would overdose on feel good hormones, but when the littlest upset occurred, like Lara ignoring a text message, Sasha would experience serious, unexplainable withdrawals. It was a fragile and precarious way to live. Sasha's lifestyle was ruined; she lost sight of true happiness and how to obtain happiness, separate from Lara.

The tight reign Lara held Sasha in was hypocritical, seeing as Lara felt comfortable cheating on Sasha with others, but wouldn't grant Sasha those same freedoms. Lara purposely avoided talks about romantic exclusivity to maintain her polyamorous lifestyle. The two never had a conversation defining the relationship and restrictions that came along with it, simply because Lara wanted to keep it as it was – open enough for Lara to pursue other people but closed enough that Sasha did not feel like she had those same rights. Sasha wasn't always the blind fool Lara saw her as. She was once strong-headed and looked up to by many, but now she was strong-headed about all the wrong things and looked up to by no one. There were, of course, instances when Sasha couldn't take the emotional stress and couldn't deny that something was seriously wrong, but inevitably, she always came back to what she had grown comfortable with – Lara's control. At the end of the day, Lara's wish was Sasha's command. This became engrained in the Sasha like a natural instinct and a compulsive habit.

Whenever the two got back together after tumultuous breakups, Sasha would always warily joke about how they would never be able to really split up, because the option of getting back together would always be there. Whenever Sasha would start to feel confident, comfortable, and safe again in the relationship, Lara would just revert back to her immature immorality. However, Sasha held onto Lara tighter and more loyally than ever. The passing of time only made the situation worse.

Lara didn't understand Sasha's "neediness," "dependency," or "attachment," but that didn't stop her from taking full advantage of these obvious yet intangible imbalances. Lara didn't stop until she had the satisfaction of knowing Sasha would do absolutely anything under the sun and moon for her. Lara knew she could move on if she wanted to, but staying certainly had its perks. She knew she was Sasha's world and that Sasha was smart and talented enough to make a fortune later on. Lara saw their relationship as a financial investment in her future, while Sasha was head over heels in love, lust, and obsession. At the end of the day, Sasha was a talented, creative, and intellectual person, but her heart began to beat so quietly that people began suspecting she had become a mindless robot.

One day, to everyone's surprise, Lara broke up with Sasha. What?! Why? No way. Lara did it on a flippant whim, and Sasha took it horribly, launching into a mental frenzy. What was life anymore - let alone school, health, and safety? Sasha entered a dangerously vulnerable state. She discovered her obsession with Lara had burned all her bridges. Lara's life became her life, so when it was taken away, Sasha felt she had nothing left to live for. All of Sasha's eggs were in Lara's basket, and Lara smashed all of them with two simple words, "it's over."

Lara's parting words triggered a dark, twisted, and confused instability within Sasha. Sasha began to hear ominous and threatening voices in private moments and didn't want to say anything about it, certain no one would understand her and worse, that they would deem her psychotic. Sasha tried to reach out to Lara, the one person she thought could help her, but these frequent, desperate attempts were all to no avail. Lara simply did not care or feel any responsibility for Sasha's well-being.

As far as the dark and deafening voices, Sasha began to not only experience intense delusions, but she also was taken over by sudden anxiety attacks. Soon, she would entertain suicidal ideation. The more Sasha tuned in to these voices, the more malicious they sounded. Either Lara could telepathically transmit thoughts into Sasha's head from afar, or Sasha had let Lara create a monster inside of herself - a monster that knew no time or distance.

Similar to a robot sleepwalking on autopilot, the overwhelmed Sasha began to both physically and mentally follow the instructions the voices were giving her. As Sasha gradually became more and more removed from what she knew, she began seeing Lara's face mouthing the words the voices spoke inside her head. One night, Sasha was too entranced in a hypnogogic hallucination to realize that she had made her way outside her apartment. Before she knew it, she was in her pajamas at the Golden Gate Bridge…she then reached both of her arms out for a warm and familiar embrace from Lara, but she felt nothing but the cold, night air.

The aftermath and trauma from the loss of a lover and friend pushed Sasha step by step to a dark and lonely demise. The last words Sasha heard as she took her last step off the bridge were Lara whispering: "Go ahead, my little robot. You can do it, just JUMP."

And the water ate Sasha whole with no mercy.

2 THE MUSIC OF THE FOREST

Today is the day! I can barely contain my excitement. I have heard countless myths about the mysterious forest and fantasized about the curious occurrences my peers claimed to have experienced there. Fortunately, my friends and I made plans to enter the forest, and I have been eagerly anticipating today for almost half a year now.

I get up before my alarm clock had a chance to ring. I go about my daily morning routine of brushing my teeth, washing my face, and hopping into my clothes for the day. Before leaving my room, I double-check that all my wilderness essentials are in my backpack: a Swiss army knife, pepper spray, bug repellent, sunscreen, water, sandwiches, matches, flashlights, and more.

As I go down the stairs, the morning bacon smells good, but I have plans with my friends that I don't plan to let my parents know about. They must have also heard countless tales about the forest, some good and some bad. Either way, the forest always brings up a sense of unpredictability and danger; thus, my parents will never allow my friends and I to wander there. I can overhear my parents making light conversation, but fortunately, they don't notice me sneak by. Taking advantage of this perfect moment, I stealthily open the side door and slip into the garage.

It's so early in the morning that the sun has not fully risen, and the garage's lack of windows makes it pitch black inside. I instinctually run my hand up the wall, searching for the light switch, and I touch the wall, which feels oddly moist, squishy and cool. I wipe my hand on my ragged old jeans. Then, when I find the light switch with the other hand, I look at my soiled hand and see the remnants of a brown slug smeared across my blue denim. Eww. I grab a nearby Lysol wipe to clean it with.

Finally, I secure a mode of transportation – my brother's bright yellow electric scooter. He hasn't touched his scooter in months. He surely will not mind me borrowing it, especially with all the stories I plan to create on it today. So, I open the garage door and head out, making sure not to turn on the engine until I was out of my parents' earshot. They wouldn't be mad that I left to hang out with friends this fine Saturday morning, but they would have opposed it if they knew our destination.

I travel down Bollinger Road, down a winding path filled with brightly colored flowers, to my cousin Jeremy's house. When I get there, I whistle to get his attention, knowing he is expecting my arrival. He looks out his window to be sure, and I whisper, "Ey homie, I'm here." Jeremy's parents also would not approve of him sneaking out to embark on a mysterious adventure with me. So, I wait for Jeremy to creep downstairs like he always does when we sneak out together, and I finally hear him in his cluttered garage. Then I hear a "meow." When the garage door opens, I see Jeremy's cat Pikachu who's hungry for food and water. Jeremy hurriedly pours some cat food on the ground before the two of us head off to his friend Carver's house. Jeremy and I travel down Johnson Avenue, past the nearby park filled with lush bushes and trees to meet Carver.

On the way, Jeremy calls his friend Carver and reminds him, "Yo, meet us at the corner of Johnson and Tilson. Jenna's still coming right?"

On speakerphone, Carver replies, "Yeah, you know my girlfriend loves stuff like this. Jenna's in for sure, see you soon."

A few minutes pass and all four of us meet at the street corner, each of our electric scooters as bright as the next.

Jenna greets everyone, "Hey guys! Are you ready or what? I've been waiting so long for this day that I haven't been able to sleep right this whole past week."

Jeremy says, "Pipe down, Jenna. You're freaking me out."

Carver smiles in adoration of his ever-eager girlfriend.

I chime in, "You guys have everything you need on you, right? Let's go!"

We all exchange one last glance at each other, before we continue traveling down Johnson Avenue together. None of us can be distracted, as we are all mentally preparing for the coming adventure. Finally, we get back on the suburban roads and travel about five miles out of Cupertino, to the edge of a forest.

The four of us pull our electric scooters over and sit there for a minute, mulling over our imminent entrance into the forest. None of us are sure what to expect.

Jenna initiates the conversation, "Some people say the forest is mysterious and haunted, but I'm not worried. I feel invincible today." In the tense silence after her words, we enjoy the last few moments of security and comfort.

Jeremy nervously twiddles his thumbs as he throws furtive glances towards the way home. Jenna can barely stand still as her breathing becomes audible. As always, Carver wears a poker face and sits still, waiting for the next command; Carver's the kind of guy that goes with the flow and rolls with the punches, regardless of the circumstances.

Out of anxiety and hesitance, Jeremy extends an arm out to pull Carver back and says, "Dude, do we have to do this? Maybe this isn't such a great idea. Let's go. It's not too late to back out. Jenna and Frederick can do this themselves. You're coming home with me."

Carver exchanges a glance with Jeremy then with Jenna and then me. He then shrugs and clamps his mouth shut. Jenna's eyes beam with excitement as beads of sweat begin to form on her nose in anticipation of the adventure ahead. Jeremy continues to shuffle his feet as a defense mechanism to the terror he feels the forest has in store for us. Carver then adjusts his backpack straps absent-mindedly as he waits for the verdict.

Jenna speaks up, "I'm tired of sitting around. Let's go!"

Carver and I nod in agreement, while Jeremy pretends he did not hear anything. The four of us ditch our scooters at the side of the road and start making our way on foot to the forest.

Even though it is now late morning, it gets dark and gloomy as the clouds begin to block the sun and as the canopy of the forest envelops us. The forest gets so hectic with various weeds that it becomes difficult to make our way, especially with no specific paths around. We stop at a stream, where Jeremy anxiously asks, "How far are we going in, anyways?" We all know at this point the best move is to not answer Jeremy. Any word we speak warrants an extra temper tantrum from him.

Jenna begins to scoop up the stream water and splash it on her face. Her fearless love for nature allows her to be carefree in the way she experiences the forest. I let the sound of the moving water soothe me as it harmonizes with the singing of the birds. Jeremy's eyes continue to dart back and forth in fear of a monster jumping out at him from any corner; in fact, just looking at him stresses me out. Meanwhile, Carver's even breathing lets me know that he remains as undisturbed and composed as ever.

Jeremy is irked by how unaffected Carver is by this whole ordeal and says, "For Christ's sake, Carver. Why you gotta be so apathetic about everything? You just sit there and meditate, waiting on other people to make decisions for you."

I then defend Carver, "Back off, Jeremy! Carver's our rock. If at any point, we are mad, sad or glad, we can look to Carver and his yellow backpack for stability and security. Start appreciating who he is just the way he is."

Jenna says, "Yeah, Jeremy. That's why I fell for him in the first place. His composure is a God-given gift."

After this mild altercation, we take off again and walk deeper into the forest, not fully knowing what to expect.

We soon come into a clearing of sorts. We have been walking for around two miles, which is long enough so that Jenna's pale face glistens with sweat. Her black hair is now sticking to her face. Carver follows closely behind her; his footprints as soft and graceful as a gazelle's. His backpack shines a fluorescent yellow, contrasting his gray personality. Jeremy, of course, lags behind a good twenty yards, dragging his legs along lackadaisically.

It is quiet, with just the rustling and crushing of leaves under our feet.

I look around, trying to assess our location.

Jenna abruptly shouts, "Hey guys! You'll never believe this. I spot a tree house just fifty yards ahead. Think there are people in there? We have to check it out!"

We all look in the direction Jenna is now pointing towards, and lo and behold, a mahogany red tree house, with boards that are nailed on, distinguishes itself from the rest of the forest. To my further delight, I notice a castle even farther ahead, "Wow guys, forget about the tree house! Do you see that castle in the distance or am I just imagining things? We gotta go check that out."

All of a sudden, a soothing clarinet noise emerges from the tree house above us. We are all immediately allured by this familiar sound; the four of us all having been in marching band at some point in our lives. I then begin instinctively walking towards the tree house to hear the music more clearly. Upon noticing this, Jeremy immediately sticks his hand out in objection.

Jeremy demands, "Where do you think you're going, Frederick?"

"I don't know, just let me go...I'm not asking you guys to come with me."

Jenna then chimes in, "Hey! If you're going, I'm going. I'm not about to miss out on this. Carver, come on," she says, as she tugs on his sleeve until he moves.

Jeremy is clearly lost in thought as he stares blankly into the ground. When he comes to, he shakes his head wildly, as if shaking away his nerves.

He then defiantly exclaims, "That's it! This is the last straw. You guys are just asking for trouble. You're all on your own from now on. I'm outta here."

I reply, "Come on, Jeremy. Don't be like this. Why do you always bail when things get uncertain? Why don't you stick it out with us? Don't you trust us? We're all good friends here, and we'll look out for each other, regardless of whoever or whatever's in that tree house."

Jenna and Carver look on with eager eyes. The next thing we know, Jeremy dramatically turns around and storms off into the distance from whence we came, muttering incomprehensible curses under his breath.

It's down to us three now, if I can even count Carver as an additional person. Carver is the kind of guy whose presence goes unnoticed at times. He is not necessarily a pushover; he just does not voice his opinion much. Fortunately, his girlfriend Jenna is particularly spontaneous and a complete adrenaline junkie. She brings out the adventurous side in him.

Recovering from Jeremy's disappearance, I nod in the direction of the tree house and Jenna immediately understands my body language. Dragging the complying Carver along, she follows my footsteps. The tree house is within sight, and the clarinet melody continues to lure me in like a siren's voice luring in unsuspecting sailors.

Once Jenna, Carver and I climb the wobbly wooden steps nailed onto the tree trunk, we reach the top. I shout out a precautionary "Hello? Is anyone there?" I then peer into the tree house and see a red fox playing a clarinet.

I mutter to myself, "Holy shit! It's a fox playing a clarinet."

Jenna and Carver simultaneously ask, "What?"

I repeated myself, "I said, holy shit! It's a fox playing a clarinet."

Jenna and Carver exchange wary glances. Carver hesitantly asks, "So, what should we do? I knew this forest would be unpredictable."

Jenna, being the risk-taker she is, prods me to keep going, "Well, say hi or something for crying out loud."

As I peer back into the tree house, I notice that the fox has sensed our presence. He is now staring straight into my eyes, but he does not stop his clarinet playing. Instead, he raises his eyebrows to invite us in. I cautiously gesture for Jenna and Carver to come on up, while still staying on guard. It is not often one sees a fox dexterously playing a clarinet. While continuing to climb up, I make a mental note to myself about where my pepper spray is in my backpack.

Carver, Jenna and I are shocked when the tree house fox opens his mouth to say, "Hello friends. To what do I owe this visit?"

Jenna immediately steps forward and fearlessly declares, "Hi! I'm Jenna and this is my boyfriend Carver and my best friend Frederick. We're just curious about what happens in this forest, since we've all heard such different stories. When did you learn how to talk and play the clarinet?"

The fox responds, "Much obliged. Call me Mr. Fox. I learned to talk as a two year old and have learned to play the clarinet at a young age as well. I'm actually in the middle of practicing for a musical audition that is to be held at the castle. Please feel free to stay and listen in to a few tunes. I'm heading out this afternoon and need to practice every tune as many times as I can until I have them all memorized."

Jenna asks, "How far is the castle? Would you mind if we tagged along?"

Mr. Fox smiles and responds, "I suppose not. It's just half a mile away.

We can get there on foot in less than ten minutes. Please make yourself comfortable while I continue practicing."

For the next few hours, we sit listening to the fox's entrancing tunes and help ourselves to tea and cookies. Once the afternoon arrives, we begin to set off for the castle on foot with our new friend, Mr. Fox.

We are glad Mr. Fox is friendly enough to include us on this exciting event. We feel like we won a VIP pass to a major happening in the forest and cannot wipe the smiles off our faces. When we get to the castle, I cannot believe my eyes. A large crowd of animals of all colors, shapes, and sizes is gathered outside, each animal carrying an instrument of their own. The excitement is palpable.

We cautiously stay by Mr. Fox the whole time, not knowing what the proper protocol for meeting animals is and if the animals are as friendly as Mr. Fox. As we meet all of Mr. Fox's other friends from the animal kingdom, they seem more wary of us than we are to them.

To ease the tension, Mr. Fox proudly and confidently booms, "I give you, Carver, Jenna and Frederick from the land of Cupertino!"

The animals timidly reply in unison, "Are they friendly?" to which the fox enthusiastically nods.

As we eagerly soak in our stimulating surroundings, I begin to notice most trees have at least one tree house in them, serving as a home for these various animals, and that animals are watching from their homes all surrounding the castle. How have I not noticed that before? This event clearly unifies the whole animal kingdom. As the auditions continue to be heard throughout the castle, our anxiety grows as we are reminded of our duty to support Mr. Fox. With each passing moment, we eagerly anticipate Mr. Fox's performance. He is nervous for no reason, seeing as his clarinet-playing talent rivals that of none other they had heard before. Occasionally sensing his nerves, Jenna beams brightly and slaps Mr. Fox on the back.

When his name is called from the castle gates, Jenna shouts, "Go get 'em, Mr. Fox!"

Jenna and I smile at each other, knowing that this moment has made our adventure magical. We have stumbled upon a gem of an event that only occurs in this wondrous forest. The brightly colored flags and decorations melt all of our fears, worries and anxieties. There is nothing but positivity here. Why have we been so scared of the unknown? A nearby giraffe keenly notices our curious expressions, "I suppose you humans don't see sights like this much?" We respond with dumbfounded nods.

When Mr. Fox's begins to perform, his audition silences everyone's hustling and bustling. Carver, Jenna and I await him outside the castle doors with our fingers crossed. None of us dare to breathe, in efforts to hear every note of Mr. Fox's performance. Sure enough, he walks out of the castle with a huge grin on his face. We have supported him until this grand moment of success! Mr. Fox will advance to the next round of auditions.

Although we have never seen anything like Mr. Fox playing the clarinet, we realize the sooner that we are able to lose our inhibitions, the sooner we can embrace a situation. Unlike Jeremy who bailed early, the three of us who stayed got to experience a taste of the forest's magic. This will forever be a fond memory that we share. With big smiles on our faces and after saying our goodbyes, we walk back to our scooters at the start of the forest and cannot wait to tell Jeremy everything that has just happened. We promise to visit Mr. Fox again for the next round of auditions.

3 CASPER

Casper is a charming, young fellow with one too many women on his arm. He doesn't look for these love interests nor does he even welcome them, seeing as he is so jaded with his disappointment of women, a curse that comes with his high standards. He does not fall in love or even feel an initial attraction to people typically speaking. However, women fall in love with him all the time. To him, love is a one-time deal. Some inaccurately view him as a womanizer, but he knows he is just as innocent as the next guy; it's not his fault when women are magnetized by his contagiously warm personality. Casper's been waiting at a local five star restaurant and has decided to take a weeklong vacation in his favorite city in the world – Hong Kong. Casper being American Born Chinese guy, is very in touch with his Chinese culture and has been anticipating this trip for a while, researching all the best spots to visit. Thus, when he embarks on this vacation alone, he knows it will be nothing short of relaxing, and he's been searching for a freedom like that for a while. He's been too caught up in his head lately.

Upon landing in Hong Kong, taking a taxi to his hotel, and unpacking his various suitcases, Casper decides to stock the mini-fridge with essential items. Thus, he walks to a nearby grocery store. As Casper rounds the corner with the baked goods, he drops a loaf of bread when he catches sight of an old friend – Kirk. Casper's initial reaction is shock; however, when he catches sight of the thin gold wedding band Kirk is sporting, he immediately feels heat rise to his face as rage consumes him, remembering how Kirk has stolen the only girl Casper has ever learned to love. Casper's heart beats faster and faster as if trying to burst out of his chest in a bloody explosion. He begins to feel pain in his jaw as he clenches and grinds his teeth together. Somehow, Casper still manages to put one foot in front of the other, approaching this nemesis seemingly head-on. Kirk, on the other hand, has not noticed Casper's presence yet, mostly because he does not expect to see anyone he knows in Hong Kong. After all, he only moved there a few weeks prior.

When Kirk turns his head in Casper's direction, a huge smile forms on his face, "Heyo, look at that! Looky there. It's Casper Ding. How are you, man? It's been so long."

Casper musters up any and all decency left in his being to dejectedly respond, "Sup Kirk. What are you up to?"

Kirk replies, "Well, Jess and I moved here around a month ago. In fact, she's just around the corner at the Chez Patrick Deli. Did you wanna say hi?"

Casper cannot help but wonder to himself how Kirk can manage to be so genuinely civil and friendly, when all he feels himself is inner turmoil and unrest. Casper mutters to himself, "I'm gonna punch this guy if he keeps up this act. I hate how happy he is. I should be in his shoes."

Kirk raises his eyebrows, "What was that? Did you say something, old pal?"

"No, no. I was just reminding myself of what was left on my shopping list."

"Listen, I don't want to be too forward, but why don't you join Jess and me for dinner tonight at our place? I'm sure she will be thrilled to see you."

Upon hearing Jess's name on Kirk's lips, Casper's heart begins to thump uncontrollably. How does she still have this effect on him? Jess cast a love spell on Casper a decade ago, and it remains as persistent and irreversible as ever; it is far from fading. In Casper's everyday life, Jess crosses his mind around three times a day on any given day...even after a decade of consistent and excessive pining and half a world's distance apart. Casper harbors a lot of lingering, bitter feelings towards Jess from the way they broke up years before. However, his desire to get personal closure overpowers his desire to spite Jess. Thus, Casper agrees to dinner.

Later that evening, Casper plugs in Jess and Kirk's apartment address into his GPS and sets off by foot. At this point, Casper keeps replaying his last fight with Jess in his head over and over again. He spat at her feet, and she threw a hair dryer at his face. It was directly after this fight that Kirk made a move on Jess, unaware that Casper and Jess were still officially an item. However, Jess took Kirk up on his offer and dumped Casper immediately. Kirk still does not know it, but he basically stole Jess right from Casper's grasp, and Casper has never attempted to rectify the situation let alone bring it to Kirk's attention.

The misunderstanding Casper and Jess share does not directly involve Kirk; their quarrel is between them two and them two alone. It is no wonder Kirk can keep himself so composed in Casper's presence. To Kirk, Casper is just another former friend of Jess'. On Casper's way to their apartment, Casper keeps reminding himself of Kirk's innocence and Jess' conniving ability to puppet men around. He cannot help but groom himself the whole way over as a means to abate his frustration; he either picks off the lint from his sport coat or smoothens out the wrinkles in his khaki pants.

Once Casper gets to their door, he marvels at how incredibly ordinary it appears to be. He expects so much more, remembering Jess' expensive taste in pretty much everything. She must have calmed down a bit since their relationship. The drab bricks that make up the outside of the building are covered in coats of dust and spider webs. Typically, apartments in Hong Kong are high-rise buildings with a modern and chic look to them. However, this one clearly has missed the memo. Casper chuckles to himself and makes a mental note to make a dig at Jess for it, "I guess seeing her again won't be that bad."

Just as Casper is about to knock on the front door, Kirk opens it and beams him a million-dollar smile. The guy is handsome. I'll give him that, admits Casper to himself begrudgingly.

Kirk welcomes Casper with hug, "Ah, it's so good to see a familiar face in these parts. Please, please come in. Jess is just finishing up her shower and will be down right away. Her sister Lana may join us as well. Lana's available by the way…and quite the looker." Casper manages an appreciative smile and follows Kirk in.

"I promise you a tour of the place after I check on the food. Jess mentioned pot roast is your favorite?"

"Yeah, actually I love her pot roast."

"Great. Take a seat in the living room and help yourself to the minibar there. We have quite the selection."

"Alright. Thanks, man."

Casper walks into the living room, as Kirk busies away in the kitchen. Their minibar is decked out with all kinds of hard liquor, mixers, beer and wine. Casper sighs with relief, "A drink is exactly what I need right now, damn." He pours himself some bourbon on the rocks and settles himself down in the nearest sofa. Noticing the photos framed all around the room, Casper decides to study up on Jess' life after their breakup.

Casper starts a running commentary on all the various pictures, most of which are of Kirk and Jess holding each other closely in what seems like a billion small honeymoons in cities around the world. "Well well well. She sure doesn't waste any time moving on, does she?"

"You say that now, but you don't know how much you broke her heart."

Casper jerks his head around to see where the voice is coming from. He was convinced he was alone, so the emergence of this voice disorients him. A woman appears from behind a closed door; she is absolutely stunning and takes Casper's breath away.

"Hi. I guess I've never officially met you, but I've heard all about you, Casper Ding. I'm Lana, Jess's sister."

"What are you doing in there and how long have you been there?"

"I wasn't trying to eavesdrop on your little soliloquy, but I have to clear up the fact that my sister did love you and that getting over you was not a walk in the park for her. I was the one that was there to buy her tissues when she ran out, I was the one that brought her pints of her favorite Ben & Jerry's ice cream, and I was the one she would cry to when she thought Kirk might not be enough. Trust me, Casper, I know exactly who you are. I'm just surprised your flock of girlfriends let you slip away to Hong Kong instead of tying you down to their bedposts."

Upon hearing these words, Casper blushes. He has still never gotten used to how his reputation as a womanizer precedes him wherever he goes. He barks at her in a way more aggressive than he means, "Listen, I'm trying to get a break here in Hong Kong, and if I like this place enough, I'll find a job here, live here, and get a fresh start. After all, I can be a waiter anywhere I want. Also, I'd like to clear the record and say that no woman has ever meant anything since your sister walked out of my life, so don't make me out to be some kind of playboy. I don't choose for people to be attracted to me. It's actually a curse."

"A curse for them or a curse for you?"

"I guess for both, since I'm unable to return the feelings most times."

"Wanna give me a shot?"

"Come again?"

"I'm single and looking."

"What a great sister you are…making the moves on your sister's ex-lover."

"Bite me."

Casper's eyes twinkle as he squints his eyes and adjusts the angle at which he sees her. The moonlight from outside falls on her hand, which is now gently stroking her thigh. She returns his gaze with a fierce intensity, with extensive time gaps between each blink. Her pupils dilate as she scans his body. Casper's heart begins to beat out of his chest. Can she hear him? He can feel beads of sweat forming on the tip of his nose, as they do whenever he feels remotely excited. Suddenly, Casper is grateful the room has dim lighting, because his cheeks are now sure to be shining a bright, hot red – the kind of red that rivals that of a ripe tomato.

As the scent of dinner wafts into the room, Lana raises her eyebrows in anticipation. Casper can feel his mouth begin to water. They meet eyes, and Lana tilts her head towards the kitchen in an inviting manner. Casper carefully moves past the sofa and into the kitchen. He walks as if he is dodging eggshells, every move as intentional as the last. Lana leans against the wall, waiting for Casper, with a powerful and commanding presence, to walk past her and lead the way. When he brushes past her, she moves swiftly behind him, fully inhaling his freshly applied cologne. She sighs inaudibly, as she has always appreciated a nicely groomed man.

As Kirk continues to busy away in the kitchen, Casper takes a seat at the dinner table and squirms in his seat until Lana grabs the chair next to him. Casper stretches his arms up in a yawn and allows his right arm to land around her body. His eyes quickly dart to her face, and he gladly returns the smile she shoots at him.

As Casper's breathing evens, he caresses her shoulder with his palm. She leans into his chest in response. They slowly break apart upon hearing Kirk's footsteps from the kitchen near the dining room. They both know it is best not to stir the waters on such a tense night. All the pent up tensions will be addressed one by one without interference of Casper and Lana's newfound spark.

Kirk walks into the dining room carrying the various dishes of food. As the aroma wafts into the room, Casper realizes his mouth is not only watering for Lana but also for the food. Pot roast is his favorite after all. Kirk takes a seat across from Casper and Lana and is completely oblivious to the sparking romance between the two.

Thus, he innocently tries to start a conversation, "Has Jess come down yet?"

Casper and Lana hastily and simultaneously respond, "No."

Just as their voices fill the air, a creaking noise from the staircase interjects. It's Jess. Casper first notices the gorgeous evening gown she has on. It is a deep blue like the ocean and flows in the air as sea breeze does. Her damp hair falls behind her, a chestnut brown. For a second, Casper loses himself in his gaze, but he's brought down to earth when Lana places her hand on his lap under the table. This is going to be interesting, Casper thinks to himself, as his focus veers back and forth.

Jess has a sharper eye for social cues than Kirk and has already considered how compatible Lana and Casper are. She has long suspected her sister may develop feelings for her charming ex-lover, upon first conversation and even upon first sight. As she approaches the dining room, Jess's eyes focus like a hawk and seem to use x-ray vision to see Lana's hand on Casper's thigh under the table. Casper shuffles warily in his seat under Jess' gaze, revealing the truth behind her suspicions.

Jess comments in an outright manner, "Well, I see you two have met. Casper, you look as sharp as ever. I'm actually glad that the hairdryer I threw at you missed your face, because that would have deprived the world and me of the eye candy known as Casper Ding." Lana squeezes Casper's leg lightly in agreement.

Kirk chimes in, "Isn't it great that we can all get together like this?

Casper, you know Lana is quite the singer."

Casper delightedly turns to his new flame and challenges her, "I might need to hear it to believe it."

Jess snarls, "There is a time and place for that, and it isn't tonight."

Kirk looks at Lana apologetically, knowing how Jess' temper can get the best of her and how she refuses to let anyone outshine her, even if it's her own little sister.

Casper begins to wonder why he ever felt attracted to such an ice queen, as the rest of the dinner is eaten in tense silence. Eventually, the sounds of smacking gums consuming the delicious pot roast and sipping noises sharing the bottle of red begin to ascend as the four exchange glances at each other and the food.

Just as they all take their last bites, Lana gasps and remembers, "My egg custard tarts are still in the car! I made them just for tonight. Let me go get them real quick. I'll be right back!" Kirk and Casper nod in response.

Casper's eyes follow her all the way out and thinks to himself, "Kirk is right...she sure is quite the looker."

Jess cannot help but notice Casper's blatant attraction to her little sister, "You like her, don't you Caspy?"

Casper daringly replies, "You're damn right, I do." With that, a bout of spontaneity seizes him as he dons his sport coat, thanks Kirk for a delicious pot roast, and chases after Lana out the door. When he sees Lana opening the trunk of her car, he rushes over to her, pulls her close to him and plants a big kiss right on her luscious lips.

Surprised by his own bravery, he continues on, "Let's ditch these bozos and get outta here. I'm taking you out dancing tonight. I know the perfect place." With that, Casper takes Lana's hand and the two take off running. With Jess and Kirk curiously looking on through their front windows, Casper and Lana speed off to their happily ever after.

.

4 AFTER ISABEL

Dear Loved Ones,
If you are reading this note, that means I have finally achieved my life goal and killed myself. That is reason for congratulations. I have done this for several reasons and hope that you can understand why. I have been nothing but a good person all my life, and yet I have found that nice people finish last.

I am convinced that Satan rules this world and has dominion over all of my loved ones, manipulating them to be evil and wicked people who have stolen my hope. I am now left without hope, when I was once filled with large amounts of faith and optimism. I wish to be able to meet God and have a conversation with him about my destiny and what it is I am meant to do with my existence. I have been studying spirituality in great depth and have found that I lack talents that other people seem to have been born with. Why would I remain here just to be inferior to others? There is no purpose in that. A futile life is not one I wish to live.

I have always felt the need to die for the sake of others. I have always been selfless and would have done anything for anyone, but it seems now that the biggest favor I can do for others is to die on my own accord. I feel that my death is necessary. I feel that I am the chosen one who is to bring goodness to this evil Earth through my suicide, just as Jesus's death rewarded mankind. If Jesus needed to die to come back, then perhaps I do too. Aren't we all supposed to be more like Jesus, anyways?

Again, I hope to meet God and have him explain to me what all my life's suffering has been about. Maybe then, I will finally understand what this has all been for. Until then, take care, and I love you all unconditionally. I have now died for you and proven my loyalty, despite it being a naïve loyalty to a completely fallen world. All I wanted was to belong and to be loved, but now I'm not so sure that's possible on an Earth like this. They say it's always darkest before the dawn...well right now it's pitch black.

Our world will be destroyed soon at the rate we're going, so a savior must lift it up from the ashes. May that savior be me and may my life not have been in vain. I have felt the weight of the whole world on my shoulders, and it is far too heavy a burden for me

IT'S ALWAYS DARKEST BEFORE THE DAWN

to carry alone. Thus, I am driven to this death without feeling love from anyone around me – a lonely, forced death for the sake of goodness. Perhaps I am foolish for loving God and being as good of a person as possible, but I know that I have died a proper death without any regrets in my life. I would rather die bravely and nobly than live a life of fear and submission.

With everything I have left,
Isabel

The police officer finished reading the suicide note and carefully placed it in a ziplock bag at the scene of the death. He had read many suicide notes before, due to suicide being a leading cause of death, but even so, it never got easier for him to do so. This one seemed far more grandiose than others he had read and couldn't help but feel struck by Isabel's words. The note was in the back pocket of a woman named Isabel who had just hung herself to death in the garage of her house.

"It always happens to the best of them, doesn't it?" The police officer rhetorically asked his partner.

His partner was busy sawing off the noose dangling from the ceiling and lowering Isabel's cold body gently to the ground as he grunted in agreement. They were both documenting the scene in written police reports as they heard a set of keys jangling then the front door opening. Isabel's sister Jamie was home. She had seen the police cars outside and frantically started running around the house to see what was wrong.

"I'd better go warn her," the police officer urgently said as he shut the door to the scene of the crime. He met a flustered Jamie in the hallway and advised her "It's best you don't go into the garage right now. Trust me, you don't want to see and not have the option of unseeing it. Stay here for now as we wrap things up."

"Officer, what are you saying? I just want to know why you're in my house. What's wrong and why are you here?"

"Here…read this," the police officer gingerly handed Jamie Isabel's suicide note.

Jamie snatched the note from the police officer, and her jaw dropped as she read the note. Her face turned white, and she collapsed against the nearest wall and slid to the floor in emotional exhaustion.

"She called us herself with her last breaths and told us to come collect her body, so that you wouldn't have to see her that way. We got here as fast as we could, but we lost her."

"Officer, can you please give me a few moments alone?" Jamie asked weakly. The police officer nodded his head in understanding and retreated to the garage. With Isabel's note firmly clutched in her hands, Jamie was in complete shock and denial, as she sat on the ground and didn't know what else to do but to breathe deeply. Jamie would've never suspected this was going to happen; Isabel always seemed to be so strong and hopeful. That goes to show, you never know when someone will take his or her own life. Jamie read the note herself over and over again; it got harder each time she read it. She knew that Isabel had always felt different from everyone else but wasn't sure why until now. Jamie scoured her memory endlessly for clues and hints that this might happen but came up with nothing. Was there something she could've done to prevent this from happening? Was it her fault for not paying closer attention to her sister? Why was this happening to her family of all families? Jamie began spiraling in her head with these haunting thoughts and knew that her life had forever changed this day. She had lost her sister and best friend.

Isabel was a 19-year-old student when this happened, and Jamie herself had just turned 23. Jamie will never forget all the vivid memories of that day.

Now, although 7 years had passed, Jamie was still as shaken as she was the day of Isabel's suicide. Grief had taken its toll on Jamie over the years. Not a day would pass without Jamie thinking of Isabel and the way she died…the way she was stolen from Jamie. Unfortunately, Jamie couldn't help but feel responsible, as she was Isabel's best friend and confidante yet didn't pick up on any warning signs prior to the tragedy. Due to this guilt, Jamie had become heavily involved in therapy sessions surrounding topics of grief and guilt. Jamie felt more alone than ever with each passing day, despite everyone's claims that it would get better if she just hung in there one day at a time.

On one particular Friday, the therapist asked Jamie how her week was, and her response was nothing out of the ordinary.

"It's been seven years now, and I still think about her every single day," Jamie monotonously stated.

"I'm very sorry to hear that, Jamie. How would you like to work on that today?" The therapist asked.

"I see her in my dreams now. I see her doing everyday things and being her everyday self. I remember back then when we lived together, she would always wake up earlier than me to make sure my morning coffee was ready for me. At dinnertime, I would always cook the meals, and she would also wash the dishes. We took turns with most other chores around the house. Now, I cook and clean alone and make that cup of coffee for myself every morning. I sit there staring at her empty chair and wonder if she's up in heaven looking down on me or still roaming around the house as a ghost. And it's not just me that misses her. I can't say if it bothers me or not for others to approach me with fond memories of her. I'm glad she is remembered, but I wish her memories didn't haunt me this much. I wish she were here living life with me like we were before she took her life. What I would give to go on one last bike ride with her or have another movie night with her. Suicide is so final, and I'm left without closure. Time hasn't given me half of the answers I'm looking for. I wish I could get inside her head and figure it all out. Maybe then, it'll be easier for me to move on and process this."

Jamie's therapist nodded in full understanding and waited for Jamie to continue, as Jamie pulled out a crumpled piece of paper with several coffee stains and tear drops on it, which had clearly been read dozens of times. It was Isabel's suicide note. Jamie couldn't make very much sense of it though she had memorized all of its contents and knew it like the back of her hand. Jamie always knew Isabel felt a higher responsibility for the wellbeing of society than other people did, but was surprised it took her so far as to take her own life. Isabel's death affected a lot of people around her, especially her immediate communities, especially her church and the charities she volunteered for.

Jamie continued to share about Isabel as often as she could as a coping mechanism, because she felt that the more she talked about Isabel, the better remembered Isabel would be, and Jamie would never want anyone to forget Isabel. It wasn't just Jamie singing Isabel's praises though. Seven years later, people were still talking about stories of Isabel's life and how gracious she was. Isabel was clearly a shining light wherever she went and earned the respect of everyone she knew. Jamie continued to explain to her therapist the depth of Isabel's involvement with all of her close loved ones and what a hole she left in everyone's hearts. Jamie acknowledged that the note was true in that Isabel was a great person with a loving heart, but the part that wasn't true was Satan's dominion over the world. Isabel had been diagnosed with schizophrenia, and she was being taken over by paranoia and delusional thoughts that had begun to run her life more than logic and reason did. Jamie felt a desperate sorrow knowing that Isabel had chosen a permanent solution to a temporary delusion.

"I just wished Isabel had spoken up more about how she felt. I'm sure there was something I could've done to prolong her life or give her the peace of mind she wanted." Jamie commented to her therapist.

"We both know it's not fair to put that burden on yourself," Jamie's therapist responded.

"There must be something Isabel's therapist could've shared with me. I know she actively attended sessions every week."

"We're all bound by confidentiality rules and could lose our licenses if we divulged any of that sort of information without the patient having signed a release of information form. I can assure you that Isabel hadn't shared any of her suicidal ideation or plans with her therapist, otherwise her therapist would have been obligated to report her to authorities as being a harm to herself."

Jamie was grateful that her own therapist was helpful in explaining the legality behind this and how it was for everyone's best that Isabel's privacy remained intact. It was clear that all Isabel wanted others to know was what little was written on her suicide note.

Jamie walked out of therapy that day feeling particularly drained and spent. It was always tiring wondering if there was something she could have done to have prevented Isabel's death or to at least have prolonged it. Jamie and Isabel were as close as sisters get, and since their parents had both passed away in a plane crash prior to Isabel's suicide, Jamie felt the heavy weight of grief overwhelming her.

Jamie herself was beginning to feel rather hopeless and wondered if she had it in her to keep going in what seemed more and more like a meaningless and unfulfilling life. More than anything, she wished she could see her parents and Jamie one last time, but that seemed possible now only if she herself somehow could visit heaven. Because of this, she began seriously considering suicide herself but didn't think she had the determination needed to complete the task. She would mentally entertain ways to do so but always found those options to be too daunting and scary to take an actual course of action. Thus, she would be stuck in the prison of her mind thinking of ways to kill herself but never actually doing so. These racing thoughts seemed to become an endless cycle of desperation and disappointment. Jamie secretly wondered if this is what Isabel went through mentally before taking her own life and felt closer to Isabel each day that passed, because she began to understand the allure of and reasons behind suicide. Maybe it ran in the family.

Jamie often avoided going into the garage by parking her car in the driveway or storing items elsewhere. She let the garage collect dust over the years. Every time Jamie entered the garage, she would get chills all up and down her spine. Because of this, the garage hadn't changed much in the past 7 years. However, when Jamie got home from therapy later that day, she went to the garage and looked up at the spot where Isabel had tied a noose to hang herself. As Jamie inspected the ceiling, she thought to herself: This is totally doable. I'm going to do this. She then began unraveling a nearby bundle of rope with more determination than ever. However, she paused and decided it would be best to write a letter of her own. She couldn't leave without providing some last words to those that would find her. Considering how much she treasured Isabel's last words, she knew the value behind leaving a note to help provide some answers for her loved ones. Her life deserved a last goodbye. Thus, she picked up a nearby pen and began jotting this down on paper:

Dear Loved Ones,
 I had to do this. I couldn't take it anymore. I couldn't live on any longer not being

able to see the face of those I love most. I need to be reunited with them, and I now leave it up to God to decide what my fate should be. Please know that I have given this choice a lot of thought, and I hope that you grieve as little as possible over me. Remember that I am in a happier place now. I've been thinking of doing this for months, and it seems like the best choice I have left. I'm sorry you have to find me like this, but please be happy for me and respect my choice. We are all free to do with our lives what we please, and this is my wish for myself.

With everything I have left,
Jamie

5 MOMMY

"But, Mommy. I don't get it. Why are there so many bad things on Earth? Did someone overpower God? Or what is God busy doing?"

Silence filled the room as Kacie's mom Lucia shook her head in disbelief at the words of her precocious five-year-old daughter. She was so grateful to have a child that questioned the world as it is as much as Kacie did. Frankly, and often times she didn't have an answer to Kacie's questions. Even if she could think of answers, she wouldn't have shared them with Kacie. The world was full of heavy stuff that wasn't going to be sorted out anytime soon, and Lucia wanted to protect Kacie from as much of reality as possible, despite Kacie's innate thirst for learning and understanding. No one's world deserved to be shattered with a few simple words, especially not a child's. Lucia wanted so much to tell her daughter the simple truth: Humans are selfish and always have been.

Instead, Lucia paused for a moment think before finally opening her mouth and calmly stating, "That's why people like you are born into existence, honey. To make a change and inspire others to follow you." Lucia said these words with a serious weight, but Kacie didn't catch it; She simply smiled and started snuggling her head into her pillow to get ready for bed.

Lucia knew that these words were far too loaded for a five-year-old to truly grasp but couldn't help but dwell on it afterwards. She reminded herself and comforted herself that the earlier she prepared her daughter to be truly someone in this world, the better it would be for her in the long run. Lucia didn't always believe in sugarcoating words, but even she herself could not explain all the evil in the world let alone articulate it properly for her daughter. The questions Kacie asked were questions that also boggled Lucia's mind as well day and night. Age doesn't always change the problems one thinks about, but the way one thinks about the problems.

Lucia and Kacie thought about similar topics but had different perspectives on them – Kacie, the mind of a five-year-olds, and Lucia, the mother who was over four times Kacie's age.

Lucia was equally nervous and excited for Kacie to be asking questions like this, because that meant Kacie was taking one step closer to fulfilling her destiny of being the great woman Lucia wanted to raise her to be. Kacie lost her father to the war in Afghanistan years ago and wondered about him often: what he looked like, what he smelled like, and what he smiled like. She had very vague memories of him and always grew closer to her mom every time Lucia would tell her a story about Daddy. Kacie always loved these stories, because Daddy always seemed like the best kind of man there could be: respectable, brave, and fierce. He was someone to be remembered, and everyone made sure she knew that. She had his eyes and his smile and wore them proudly. Lucia was being the best a single mom could be, balancing work and a home life. Kacie was doing well for her age: excelling in school, ice-skating in her free time, making lots of friends, and being helpful to her mom.

The next morning, Lucia woke up and dropped Kacie off at school just like normal. Little did she know, it would be quite the tumultuous day. After dropping Kacie off, Lucia went to work. She was a call center agent for a nonprofit organization, nothing special but it paid the bills. Her job mainly entailed receiving telephone calls from people who wanted to donate to her company. She enjoyed her job enough, and it was close to both home and Kacie's school. On her lunch break, she had a normal routine of heating up her lunch in the microwave at work and then walking to her car to eat her meal in the car in privacy. This day like on most other days, she turned on the radio and began listening to the news. She had just started eating her spaghetti and meatballs when her jaw dropped at what she was hearing. Apparently, there was a shooter holding students hostage at the school Kacie attended. Lucia went into a panic attack. Frantic questions started popping up in her head: Where was Kacie? Was she safe? Lucia hoped Kacie wasn't doing something courageous or dangerous; she hoped Kacie was laying low and staying under the radar, but at the same time, Lucia knew that Kacie didn't have a shy or timid bone in her body. Visions of Kacie being hurt flashed through Lucia's mind, but she shook these thoughts and tried her best to get as much information out of the radio report as possible.

The news report continued on with the little information they had. They knew what the shooter looked like, because he apparently was in full communication with the police, announcing his every move and making his intentions public. On the radio, the principal was making a statement that the shooter had a whole classroom full of students locked up and barricaded in. The shooter already had a target in mind, and this target was in the said classroom. One of the student's mothers owned a special crystal that could make anyone not only invincible but also immortal. The mother had this crystal locked away in a safe and was able to obtain it through inheriting it from a long line of family members. It was a prized possession. Though she owned the stone, she did not directly wield its powers, nor had any of her ancestors, because the stone only worked if the person who wielded it was fit for it, otherwise the person would be obliterated immediately. In this case, the shooter knew that he had it in his blood to withstand the power of the stone, because he was a part alien, and it was the exact alien species needed to withstand the crystal's impact and power. In fact, he was half-reptilian, and it showed. His skin was slightly greener than usual, and his skin complexion was scaly, like that of a crocodile or lizard. He had come from his home planet on a UFO for the sake of landing on Earth to find the stone and bring it back to his home planet.

All of this was being reported live on the radio, and Lucia completely lost her appetite as she desperately tried to figure out what to do. She felt helpless, and the situation was beyond her. If the shooter was an alien from another planet, then what chance did she stand to protect her baby girl? Aliens were known to be a powerful force at the time, and they had just started landing more frequently on Earth for its valuable natural resources. Their encounters were always hostile, because they always wanted something from Earth, something their home planets did not have, like this stone.

Lucia couldn't help but picture the worst-case scenario – that Kacie was in that very classroom the shooter was holding hostage. She tried to think of whose mother could be the one with the stone, but it could have been any of them. Lucia got out of her car and went straight to her boss's office, requesting the rest of the day off due to this family emergency. She then drove over to the school, wanting to be closer to the whole situation. She knew where Kacie's classroom was and hoped that that wasn't where the police were surrounding. As she pulled into the school parking lot, she noticed police were crowded around a classroom at the other end of the school and breathed a deep sigh of relief. Hopefully this meant Kacie was not in danger.

Hours had passed, and Lucia still remained there at the scene of the hostage, alongside many other worried parents and neighbors. Everyone wanted to see what was going on and what progress was being made. Fortunately, students and teachers who were safe were being evacuated from the school. Lucia looked through the crowd to find her daughter, and sure enough, there she was. Lucia was overjoyed and ran over to pick her up and hug her. Kacie never felt lighter in her arms. Lucia checked Kacie for any wounds or injuries.

"Honey, I've been worried sick. I can barely breathe. Are you okay?

Are you hurt?" Lucia asked.

"Mom I'm fine, but we need to figure out what to do about my friends in that classroom," Kacie maturely responded.

"What do you think they should do? Hand over the stone and let this reptilian become all immortal and invincible or sacrifice the lives of everyone in that classroom?" Lucia probed.

This question troubled Kacie, as she had clearly given it a lot of thought. Lucia herself didn't know the right answer to the question.

Kacie then spoke up, "I think it's best he doesn't get his hands on the stone and cause more damage than he would without it, even if it means a certain amount of deaths. That would be the best approach. To save as many lives overall as possible, though it is very sad that some of my closest friends are in that classroom right now."

The honesty and maturity of Kacie's answer struck Lucia deeply, and she knew deep down that she agreed with this answer.

"Mommy, what can we do to help my friends?" Kacie looked up at Lucia expectantly.

"Nothing for now, sweetie. Now, let's go home and try to think of something else today," Lucia said.

Lucia knew that Kacie wouldn't be able to stop thinking about this until the situation was resolved, but she desperately wanted to distract Kacie from the ugly truth. Lucia felt angry and frustrated knowing that something so tragic was happening directly to Kacie's friends in that captured classroom, but she didn't know what else to do but to take Kacie home. The police were already doing everything they could to handle the situation, but they didn't stand a fighting chance against this alien.

Lucia and Kacie got into their car and headed home for the day. On the way home, Lucia kept tapping her fingers on the steering wheel out of anxiety, and Kacie kept bouncing her leg up and down. Both of them were out of sorts, though Lucia tried to remain as calm and rational as possible as a mother figure.

"Mommy, would it help to pray right now?" Kacie asked.

"Honey, it's always a good time to pray. You know that," Lucia responded.

"Okay. Father God. I pray that you save my friends in that classroom and bring them out of their misery. I pray that you protect the crystal from the perpetrator and make sure that it belongs in the hands of those who are responsible enough to wield it. I pray for all the police that are on site trying to handle the situation. I also pray that you send us more help. If there are bad aliens out there coming down to Earth to harm us, there must be good aliens out there coming down to help us. Thank you for listening, Heavenly Father. In your son's name I pray – amen," Kacie finished her thought.

Lucia began tearing up, clearly moved by Kacie's prayers. When they got home, it was dinnertime. Lucia prepared sausages, green beans, and mashed potatoes for dinner. Kacie was quiet the whole time, which was very unusual for her. Lucia then watched Kacie brush her own teeth and tucked her into bed. Lucia sung a lullaby for Kacie until Kacie closed her eyes and fell asleep. Perhaps Kacie was simply faking sleep so that Lucia didn't have to keep singing the lullaby. They both knew no one was getting good rest that night. Lucia didn't want Kacie to sleep alone in her room that night, so after Kacie fell asleep, Lucia carried her to her own king-sized bed and tucked Kacie in there. That was the only way Lucia would get any shut-eye that night, knowing Kacie was safe right there next to her.

The next morning, Lucia and Kacie got up to the morning alarm. Lucia turned the TV on immediately to see what the status was at school and if Kacie needed to attend school or not. To their surprise, the news channel reported that several alien UFOs were hovering over the school and had beamed all 30 of the students up to safety. The police had successfully captured the reptilian with the help of these new aliens. Apparently, another alien species came to help a few hours after Lucia and Kacie left the scene the day before. They placed a tracker on the reptilian and followed his UFO to Earth. He was a wanted criminal by the Galactic Federation.

Lucia and Kacie couldn't believe their eyes and jumped up and down with joy.

"Mommy! I'm so glad we prayed. Our prayers have been answered."

"They sure have, sweetie. They sure have."

"I wonder where the crystal is now."

"I'm sure it's right where it belongs. All is well again."

Kacie couldn't wait to go to school to see the scene. She knew there wouldn't be class, but she wanted to celebrate this happy ending with her freed classmates. Thus, Lucia drove Kacie to school to see everyone. When they got there, there was a crowd of other cars who had come to witness the miracle. Most of them were newspapers and journalists trying to document the moment, but it was clear that the families of the students were in the cars as well – crying with relief.

6 THE SILVER RINGS

She instinctually stares at the glistening, silver ring resting on her lap until her tears dry, and her eyelids become heavier and heavier with the passing moments. She slips the ring back on her left ring finger and sighs to herself as she sluggishly looks around at the familiar darkness that engulfs her, body and soul. Never did she think she would find a love as torturous or rewarding as this one or one that crushed her to the extent of this one. She dejectedly mumbles softly to herself, "Jane...that's right. That's right, my name is Jane. Hi, my name is Jane. Hi...hello." Reminding herself of her name always helps when she becomes consumed in thought. Ruminating over the breakup never drifted far before consuming Jane all over again. The devilish traps of her own mind steal her connection to reality, forcing her to weave in and out of glooms of depression. When Jane reluctantly acknowledges that she has done enough mulling for the day, she gets up from her mundane, green couch and begins digging for answers of the past through old storage boxes, all the while reminiscing about how she and her fateful former friend first met in college. College, of course, is the romantic time when everyone begins capriciously experimenting sexually or in Jane's case, begins courting to find a serious soul mate.

As Jane mulls around her house examining each of her stacks of brown cardboard boxes, she can't help but notice the ones that are carefully labeled with Payton's name. These are the only ones that lack a layer of thick dust over them – the ones with multiple, desperate handprints from frequent opening. She trails her fingers over Payton's name on the closest box and can't help but tear up a little, mostly realizing how sorry she feels for herself. It's been twenty years since they parted ways, but the grief has aged Jane immensely.

To this day, Payton means the world to Jane, but to Payton, Jane lost all value when she no longer had an Adderall prescription. This shook Jane, because either he was the best con artist ever or she was a complete fool. Both options were gravely disappointing, seeing as she always prided herself in her good judge of character. Anyone would have been fooled - they would sit next to each other in every class, hang out outside of campus, and travel to each other's hometowns to meet. It was also the way Payton smiled every time he saw her. She could have sworn he was in love with her, so naturally, she thought graduation would mean a new chapter of life for both of them. She wanted new levels of commitment. She wanted it all with him. She wanted Payton to see her as a life partner; however, her reasonable hopes were quickly and brutally shattered.

After graduation, Payton wanted to make Jane feel as small as he could. Thus, he made the traitorous move of telling the police that she was abusing her Adderall prescription and forcing him to take it with her, which was far from the truth of her giving him free Adderall whenever he wanted it. He used her voicemails, texts, emails, and letters to incriminate her, claiming that she was harassing him and that she would not leave him alone. With the help of the local police and civil court, he filed a restraining order against her.

Jane loved Payton so much that she confirmed all of his false accusations and suffered the punishment for them – never being able to contact him or see him again.

As Jane opens one of the boxes, various trinkets, souvenirs, and receipts remind her of their distant past together. She always gave Payton the benefit of the doubt, and her love for him drove her forgiveness for him.

She trips over a glass ornament meant for a Christmas tree, and suddenly a wave of frustration washes over her. It was as if all of her passive aggression was catching up to her in that instant. As she picks up the glass ornament she tripped over, she quickly pivots to the nearest wall she could find and shatters the glass sphere against it. A rush of energy surges within her as copious amounts of blood begin oozing out of her hand and wrist. It's like she finally feels something from years of dormancy. She feels her feet unable to support her weight any longer as she loses consciousness and faints.

As Jane comes to again after what seems like days, she hears the beeping of a heart monitor, feels a warm hand on her forehead and tastes a salty teardrop freshly fallen on her lips. She feels life inviting her back into the world, but struggles accepting the invitation. Moments later after a battle with her consciousness, Jane realizes it's probably for the best that she wakes up and faces reality. Time to face the music and do damage control. She knew she must be in the hospital due to the bright lights she could detect from behind her closed eyelids, the sound of her heart being monitored on a nearby machine, and the smell of funky hospital food.

Just as Jane decides to open her eyes, she feels the wind of someone rushing into the room. The scent of this person is so familiar that it stirs something within her and causes her eyes to jolt open. Her vision is blurry, and as she fumbles around for her glasses, which she usually keeps attached to a neck strap, she hears a crisp, clear, and confident voice booming:

"Hi! I'm Jane's emergency contact. I'm here. It took me a few hours to get here, but I'm here," the voice boomed confidently. "Tell me she's okay. Tell me I can talk to her. Tell me she's alive! I'm sorry. Where are my manners? You're Jane's nurse, right?" After waiting for the nurse to process his words and nod, the voice continued, "My name is Payton. Payton Connor. I would like to know her complete status."

Jane's nurse smiled gently and knowingly, having guided many conversations with worried emergency contacts in the ER. "Honey, relax. She's fine," she reassures Payton, "Actually, it seems like she's coming to." As she nods in Jane's direction, she continues with a wink, "I'll give you two a few moments alone."

Payton looks over at Jane and forgets the nurse is in the room, as he walks over to Jane's hospital bed. He begins, "Why am I still your emergency contact? You really haven't changed a bit. You've always been a recluse and a hermit." He can't hold back a chuckle to relieve the tension, "Who would've thought you never bothered to change your emergency contact information after all this time? Well, I'm happy to be here. I'm happy to see you again."

Jane goes along with the conversation, knowing full well it is most likely a delusional fantasy from the painkillers she's on.

"Hi Payton."

An amused Payton asks, "Is that all you have to say?"

Jane starkly replies, "Yes, until you explain yourself."

"You know I always wanted you, but I wanted you to fight for me. I wanted you fight back," Payton begins explaining, "I wanted you to show me something I needed to know, which was whether or not you could live without me...for you to show me that I was all that you truly wanted. I knew that to stir something within a strong-headed person like you required a big move, a strong gesture, a powerful yet risky act. I lifted the restraining order years ago, out of a small hope you would think to find me again – that you hadn't forgotten me."

Jane smirked, letting her denial melt away and beginning to grasp the situation.

Finally after what seemed like hours of pained silence, she said, "Look what I still wear everyday."

She flashed the silver ring on her left ring finger that she often looked at in times of deep sadness.

Payton smiled back, responding "Don't think I don't still have mine," as he takes out his wallet out of his back pocket and pulls out a matching silver ring from inside of it.

They had swapped friendship rings years ago as a promise to each other to stay friends. Jane was more than happy to restore her faith in what they had.

Jane admits, "Just as I was starting to give up on you, here you come, swooping in to save the day like the Superman I always knew you were. Don't you dare think that this is good enough of an apology for all these years lost."

Payton responds, "Well, that depends. Have you learned your lesson by now? Have you learned how to fight for what you want?"

Jane responds, "Sure, how about we start with this?" She then promptly punches him right in the gut.

Payton snorted the way he always used to when he couldn't contain a laugh and said, "That'll do for now."

7 PROFESSOR WASHINGTON

Trigger Warning: Heavy sexual content
"Well I'm the only professor who teaches this class, so you better suck my dick good and hard if you want a chance at passing," Professor Washington seethed at Katya.

They were alone in his office, as they often were. Professor Washington demanded these office hour appointments with Katya to allow for private playtime for the two of them. Katya had a severe learning disability that made it difficult for her to understand class material. Though she had academic accommodations from the university's disability resource center, the accommodations weren't nearly enough to compensate for the slower rate at which she learned. The professor was well aware of this deficit every time he graded another paper or exam of hers. At the same time, he knew that Katya would be willing to trade sex for grades as a result of her dire situation. He had gotten to know Katya well over the quarters; this was not his first time having her in his class. The risk of getting caught didn't cross the professor's mind. He led with his lust without thought for the repercussions of his actions. He would rather continue his great secret tradeoffs with Katya than maintain his unblemished reputation as one of the most popular professors on campus.

Katya was a beautiful, beautiful young woman. Her long black hair, tan skin, and athletic physique made her look graceful, elegant, and well put together. She was the kind of person that people's jaws would drop at. Most guys did double takes when they saw or met her for the first time, in disbelief of her good looks. She, of course, was blind to her own beauty. In some twisted way, she found Professor Washington attractive, whether it was the power dynamic or his charisma. This made the sexual favors worth the great recommendation letter that he promised her as well as the consistent A's he started giving her on assignments. She didn't even have to turn anything in anymore.

Katya will always remember the first time Professor Washington seduced her. Oddly enough, she had just started fantasizing about him sexually when he would prolong their eye contact in class or look her up and down noticeably. It seemed like every time Professor Washington saw Katya, he would lick his wrinkled lips and hope to see up her skirt. Katya didn't know why she was thinking about Professor Washington in this way, when he was double if not triple her age…perhaps it was the way he demanded her attention in class. If she ever looked away from him to glance out the window, he would call her out in the middle of class:

"Katya, is there something outside of the classroom that's more important to you right now?" He would ask in front of everyone.

These were clearly biased questions, seeing as less attractive students would leave the classroom to use the restroom or take phone calls without him even noticing.

Katya and Professor Washington had known each other for two quarters now, and every time she visited his office hours, he would demand more. This particular day, he wanted a blowjob. He impatiently awaited Katya's answer to his blatant request.

"Can we please not record it this time? My boyfriend would kill you if he ever saw the footage," Katya pleaded.

"I've told you so many times, cupcake. The videos are for my wife, so she can learn how to look like you and please me like you do. And now, she can learn to suck like you do. The more sucking she does, the less sucking you have to, so let's go. We don't have all day. I have a meeting after this so come on," Professor Washington restlessly explained as he turned on the video camera in his hands and set it up on a tripod nearby. "I want you to do it as well as you know how, as well as you suck your pretty little boyfriend's cock. And if I don't feel how badly you want me, you're gonna be happy to do it again next week."

Katya nodded silently, fully understanding the task in front of her. She tied her hair in a ponytail and dropped to her knees while discreetly locating the wall clock in his office to keep track of the time. If she could get him to ejaculate as soon as possible and get it down to a system, then everything would be okay – there would be a science behind it, and she could clock out in her head as the minutes unfolded. She warily reached her hands out to take off his belt and unbutton his pants. She knew this was it. They were crossing all kinds of boundaries here, but if she didn't get a passing grade in this class, she would have to take out student loans for another school year, which she just couldn't afford at the time. Giving him a 5-10 minute blowjob was so much better than spending 5-10 hours on weekly homework assignments, especially when she would likely still fail turning in her own assignments and have to pay for another quarter's tuition just to retake this one class.

While she undid his pants, she kept trying to picture her boyfriend Jake in her head by closing her eyes, but she couldn't block out the stench of Professor Washington. He clearly hadn't showered that day or maybe even for the past few days. As she pulled out his member, she wanted to gag at his body odor. But, she was a strong girl and resisted her own disgust. She had to do what she had to do. As she began running her cold hands up and down his warm shaft, she realized that this was the first time she had seen or felt his penis. She wondered if she was special to him or if there were other students tending to his needs. She secretly hoped she was the only one. She felt a sense of pride and power, knowing that he wanted her sexually. This was a privilege not all students had...trading sex for class credit. Suddenly, she stopped noticing his body odor and started realizing how beautiful his penis was. It was all hers, for the time being.

For some strange reason, Katya couldn't wait to put it in her mouth. She wondered if she could please him the way he wanted. She first tentatively probed the tip of his penis with her tongue. It tasted slightly salty, just the way Jake's did. Professor Washington bucked his hips in response, wanting so badly to feel her warm mouth around all of him. She pulled back. She was teasing him. She wanted to enjoy this now. In her head, she couldn't decide if she secretly resented him for abusing his power of if she was grateful for the opportunity to cheat her way to an easy A. Convincing herself of the first option clearly helped her sleep better at night. Up to that point, she would lie awake thinking of the way they kissed or the way they held each other, but today meant something different. Today meant having sex, oral sex. Katya opened her mouth to allow him access. Their bodies were in sync. Well, her mouth and his groin at least. Professor Washington began grunting wildly and uncontrollably as Katya's lips and tongue worked their way around his member at a faster and faster pace. The sounds of loud sucking and choking filled Professor Washington's office until he aggressively slapped her face to get her attention. She looked up in betrayed dismay to find him holding his finger to his mouth to remind her to keep the noise down. His office was surrounded by other professors' offices, and the walls were thin – paper-thin. This made Katya feel less than special, as she began wondering if this was common practice for him and if he knew exactly how well sound traveled.

After Katya quieted down her rhythmic sucking, Professor Washington started to really let himself savor the moment. It's not often a 60-year-old professor finds his penis inside a beautiful and blossoming young woman. For more comfort, he changed from his standing position to being seated by guiding his left hand from the back Katya's head toward him as he leaned back in his black, leather chair. He grabbed the camera off of the tripod and held it in his right hand instead. The entire time adjusting, Katya masterfully understood his body language and never disengaged his penis from her mouth. He began playing with her breasts from underneath her shirt as a reward.

He realized how much better he liked this position, because now his stomach wasn't blocking his line of sight, and he could clearly see Katya working her head up and down with every other beat. He grew more and more comfortable with the passing moments, as the anxiety of getting caught faded from his head. Clouded with lust, he began barking orders in the form of whispers at Katya for more, harder, faster. Just as Professor Washington was hoping it would never end, he ejaculated into her mouth. The urgency in his dilated pupils let Katya know that she was meant to swallow if she wanted to do it right. She wasn't going to turn back now, so she complied, gulping down his natural juices.

They checked the clock at the same time, exchanged a glance, then started grooming themselves to prepare for the world outside this office. Professor Washington instinctually started pulling out his wallet and reaching in for some cash.

"That'll do, here's your…Oh wait, I forgot you're not one of my whores. You'll get paid differently." He bluntly remarked as he put his wallet back into his back pocket.

Katya pretended this didn't happen, not wanting to know how many people she was sharing him with. As she watched him dress, she began to notice for the first time how old he looked. He had liver spots covering his groin area, huge wrinkle lines down his face, and long, stray hairs coming out of seemingly everywhere. He looked much older than he said he was, or maybe he had lied about his age.

After the professor put away his camera, he opened his office door and signaled for her to leave. No words were exchanged as she left his office. Katya quickly looked up and down both directions of the hall, grateful to find that the coast was clear. She knew she had two more classes before her long day would finally end. By the end of her last class, she couldn't wait to get back to the comfort of her own bed.

On the bus ride home, Katya kept thinking about how much she wanted to shake off the memories of the past hour, brush her teeth, and listen to soft music. Prior to the fellatio, she and the professor had a lengthy and familiar discussion about the risks of her not passing the class and the consequences she would face upon failure of the course. Katya couldn't afford any mishaps, which led to the professor's bold and lascivious request. Katya had to come up with a quick decision and ultimately agreed to his demands. They had never crossed that line before. Prior to that, it was always her agreeing to let him film her flashing him her breasts, performing stripteases, or allowing some light touching. In retrospect,

Katya was pleased with her choice and felt that sexual favors were more than worth the trade off for everything she would gain from being under Professor Washington's wing.

It was early evening when Katya finally got back to her dorm building after what felt like an extremely long day. Just as she plopped herself on her bed for some much-needed rest, her phone started buzzing. She sluggishly glanced at the screen to see that Jake was calling her. She immediately ignored the call. A few moments later, her phone started buzzing again. Jake again. It was then that she noticed Jake had texted her five times, which she found odd, because Jake usually didn't like texting. So, Katya picked up the phone.

"Babe, what?! I'm so exhausted right now, I can't talk." Katya mumbled into the phone.

"What the fuck is this?" Jake snapped viciously.

"What's what? Listen, can we talk later? I'm super tired and can't really think straight right now," Katya replied.

"No – we need to talk RIGHT NOW!" Jake shouted.

But Katya had already hung up the phone in exhaustion. She then decided to at least browse through his texts to see what the hullaballoo was all about.

"Holy shit. No way…this can't be happening…" Katya whispered to herself. Suddenly, she jolted herself awake. Jake had sent her a screenshot and a link to a porno video of her and Professor Washington.

She frantically wondered to herself how this was possible when it dawned on her that the professor had recorded the whole thing. Jake's text messages read: "TELL ME this isn't happening." "TELL ME this isn't you." "TELL ME this isn't what you were doing when you told me you had to meet with him today for office hours." "TELL ME you weren't wearing the exact same outfit the chick in this fucking porno is." "TELL ME that's not the exact flower tattoo you have on your left breast."

Katya's heart began racing as she watched the excruciatingly embarrassing video. She couldn't believe that he was able to upload this video, blur their faces, and post it by the time Katya finished classes and got home. Had he been posting all of the videos all along? She was grateful he took the time to censor the video, but ultimately, Katya felt furious…mostly because Jake wouldn't trust her anymore, and she loved Jake more than anything.

Thus the next day, she decided to go straight to Title IX. She was determined to report Professor Washington for sexual harassment, and her university's Title IX office was exactly the right place to go for that. After making an urgent phone call to them, Katya found out she was able to drop by for a walk-in appointment that same day. She then hopped on the next bus that would take her there. On her bus ride, she ran through various scenarios in her head about how the meeting would go, what she wanted to reveal, and how much trouble she wanted Professor Washington to be in. She hopped off the bus and hastily followed a campus map on her phone to the Title IX office.

Katya walked into the Title IX Office and quickly noticed how bare its gray walls were - no flyers, no announcements, no activities, nothing. She also noticed how quiet and deserted it was – no secretary, no assistant, no noise, nothing. She began to get cold feet. Will they even care? What do I expect out of this? How does Title IX even work? Just as Katya was feeling in over her head, she saw a silver call bell and rang it before she could change her mind.

Ding!

Seconds later, a Title IX investigator wearing a gray dress suit, thick-rimmed glasses, and shiny shoes approached Katya.

"Hello there. You must be Katya. We've been waiting for you. Please come this way."

"Thank you, sir." Katya replied as she followed him down a hallway that echoed their footsteps.

As they rounded the corner, a room with an open door came in sight. They walked into the room. Inside the room, to Katya's surprise sat Professor Washington…his legs comfortably crossed and his hands cradling a cup of hot coffee.

"What is he doing here?" Katya gasped in objection as she sharply turned to the Title IX investigator.

The Title IX investigator responded by gesturing politely to Professor Washington to allow the professor to explain. The professor then broke the tense silence with a hearty laugh at her dismay.

"Cupcake, cupcake, cupcake" he started saying as he shook his head gently. "The Title IX investigators here on campus are my good friends and have been for a long, long time. Now, we can either do this the hard way or the easy way…Are you sure you want to make any false allegations against me? And before you utter a word, I will say that out of the warmest regards for you, I strongly advise you not to."

Katya stood there in disbelief, hoping that the passing seconds would help strengthen her resolve to do the right thing. She looked hopefully at the Title IX investigator for help or comfort, but he simply stood there, unmoving and expressionless.

"What do you think my emergency meeting was about yesterday, cupcake? I had to come say hi to my friends here," he continued. "In fact, George, would you mind leaving us alone for a few moments? I need to speak to her in private, please."

The Title IX investigator nodded, winked, and left the room briskly. The next thing she knew, Katya heard the door lock behind the Title IX investigator from the outside, leaving just her and Professor Washington in the room. Professor Washington then sighed as he pulled out his video camera, turned it on, looked at her, and began unbuttoning his pants.

"Let's go, cupcake. We don't have all day. I have a meeting after this so come on, you know what to do." Professor Washington barked.

Katya then dropped to her knees, tied back her hair, and began sucking his dick with more enthusiasm than ever.

8 THE COLORS OF OUR SOULS

"Push, push! It's almost out. Just a few more pushes, and we're there," the doctor said as he guided the baby out of its mother.

A few moments later with a piercing cry, the baby announced its presence in the world. The doctor allowed himself to be briefly vulnerable as he stared at the baby in awe. New life was always a wonder to him, despite his profession. He then swiftly passed the baby to its mother before remembering the rest of his job. He grabbed a nearby scanning device. Naturally, he had quite a few lined up next to each other.

"Are you ready for its Soul Determination?" The doctor sympathetically asked the mother, knowing how much weight these words held.

"Just a few more seconds" the mother requested.

"We don't have much time. They'll be coming any moment now if they don't receive its color." The doctor urged her.

The mother gave an austere nod, and the doctor wasted no time in scanning the baby with his handheld device. The device was sleek and simple with three brightly colored circles that each lit up: red, yellow, and green. When the doctor pushed the only button on the device, a line of white light covered the entirety of the baby's body up and down. Then the doctor held the scanner inches from the baby's heart until the scanner started beeping wildly.

After the loud beeping subsided, the third circle lit up bright and hot – it was the red one. The scanning device announced austerely, "Red. This baby is red."

"NOOOOOOOO!! NOT MY BABY! NOT MINE!" The mother screamed.

"It must be done for the Queen." The nurses nearby said in unison. The head nurse then passed the doctor a tube filled with white viscous liquid. The tube was labeled with one word "Justice."

The doctor then promptly turned to the baby and squeezed the inner material of the tube all over the baby's face, with special attention to fill up the baby's nostrils, mouth, and ears. It acted like superglue, sealing the baby's ears, eyes, nose, and mouth all tightly shut, as the baby suffocated to death. All the while, the mother could not stop screaming. Then, the doctor apathetically signaled for the nurses to wheel the mother out of the room.

"It's always difficult when the mothers don't understand." The doctor calmly explained to the nurses as he shook his head in disappointment. He proceeded in a calm fashion, "Would any of you like to see the damage we have saved the world from facing? This is always my favorite part."

The nurses turned to each other, smiled, and nodded. A treat like this was not common. They had had a long day, and the doctor felt the need to reward them. So, he cut a slit on the flesh of the baby's underarm, collected a drop of the blood on a metal chip, and inserted the chip into the scanning device he used to determine the baby's soul. The scanning device then flickered on again. Instead of the white light originally used to scan the baby, the device now projected a movie of what would've been the baby's life, only it picked out the highlights...and these highlights were extremely gruesome. The movie revealed that the baby would go on to commit egregious acts of violence. At 5 years old, he found a raccoon in his backyard and skinned it alive for fun. At 8 years old, he made his best friend suffocate to death by intentionally giving him banana nut bread that allergically closed his throat. At 13 years old, he stole his best friend's girlfriend's virginity. At 18 years old, he ran over a dark-skinned man at night. At 23 years old, he convinced his girlfriend of two years to commit suicide. After seeing all of this in rapid succession, the nurses decided they couldn't take any more and asked the doctor to turn off the device, which he gladly did. The scenes were vivid and thorough, though only lasting minutes long.

Hours later in the room next door, the mother was waiting to be discharged from the hospital. She was washed up and ready to go. Despite the nurses' pleads for her to stay the night to heal and get some rest, she insisted on gathering her belongings and getting out of the whole scene. She wanted to get back out in the world and create a new life for herself, one apart from her lost baby. As she progressed through the next few months of her life, all of her loved ones tried their best to console her in different ways. The most remarkable piece of advice she got was from one of her best friends, who advised her to visit a nearby store of witchcraft and wizardry. Apparently, they sold healing stones and crystals there that could spiritually help with both her broken heart and physically help her with her body's recuperation process. She decided this was good enough of an idea, searched online for the nearest store that carried such items, and found one in the downtown of her town. The place was called The Kiss of Life.

As she arrived at the store, the mother immediately spotted the shop owner and introduced herself to him, as she frequently did when entering a new store. She could always spot the owners by the way they commanded a presence in the stores.

"Hi there! I'm not really sure what I'm looking for, but I was told to come here for something to help me heal. I gave birth to a red baby. I would've given anything to have given birth to a yellow like myself or even a green." She said as she began to approach the storeowner.

"Ah, I'm very sorry to hear of your loss. I suppose you'll be wanting a crystal then?" The shop owner asked her.

"Yes. I would like a crystal not just for healing but also to guarantee my next baby's a green one." The mother began to say with more confidence.

"I'm sorry to say that there is no way to manipulate the Soul Determination of a child. All the witchcraft, wizardry, magic, sorcery, and whatever else in the world cannot guarantee you a green child. You need to earn it by healing yourself completely first. Why don't we start with a reading of your chakras and auras? My crystal ball is right in the back, and I do it on a donation basis. I can tell you're in distress, and it's a slow day here in the shop…and more importantly, I would like to help." The shop owner looked at her with sympathetic eyes, and she knew he was sincere.

"Sure, I mean I don't believe in all that mojo stuff, but I suppose it wouldn't hurt to try." She gave in.

"Good, good. Why don't we step in the back…there's quite a bit you need to know, and I would love for your permission to tell you all about yourself." The shop owner royally waved his hand towards a back room. The mother raised her eyebrows in suspicion but managed to put one foot in front of the other to approach the room. She was fully expecting for him to lead her into a disheveled and dilapidated room with nothing in it but dust; however, when he opened the red curtains for her to walk through, she couldn't help but gasp when she saw how beautiful the room was. Perhaps it wasn't just that, perhaps it was the energy and aura filling the room. It was a holy place, and she knew it immediately. A spiritual high began emerging inside of her, and she began to look at the storeowner with much less skepticism and much more wonder.

"Where am I?" She meant it more as a whisper to herself, but he smiled in reply.

"I'm about to tell you if you'll let me. Give me your permission, and I'll tap into one of my six healing guides to help you. This is my room of healing. It's not unusual for you to react this way. You'd be surprised what's happened to people once they've set foot in this room or spent time in this room. With the incenses burning, the deities watching, and the spirits I've channeled in here, I've done everything I can to make this room this room."

"Okay…" The mother said as she began to doubt her trust in this man again. She was experiencing a serious case of information overload. She had never really trusted in the supernatural before, but this seemed like a good first chance to.

The storeowner smiled again, this time more warmly and convincingly.

"Please have a seat. In a moment, you'll be able to ask me anything you want. Give me a few seconds to tune into the crystal ball." He said to her as he lit a sage incense and waved it in the air, letting it waft all around his crystal ball. She made herself comfortable and sat down when she saw how absorbed he was into tapping into the crystal ball. He ran his hands over all sides of the ball, expertly and smoothly. He looked deep into the crystal ball, as if he was looking across all the stars in the universe. In that instance, she knew he was real – that this was not a gimmick. She knew there was more to her story than she knew and that he could help her. A man rarely gets a look like that on his face – a look of omniscience.

"Well, if you don't mind, I think I'd rather start with a more human introduction. I'm assuming you're a wizard of some sort?" She chimed.

The storeowner looked up from his crystal ball as though she had interrupted a very deep and intimate moment. After registering her question moments later, he finally responded, "You could say that, yes. You could definitely say that."

"Okay, well. My name's Abigail, and I'm a yellow."

"I'll stop you right there. I hate to be the first one to tell you this, but you're actually a green. But, I will say that this was a fortunate mistake and that your whole life thus far has not been lived in vain."

"That's impossible. I would've been sent to the academy. I was paired with a green immediately and ended up marrying him. Unfortunately, he passed away not too long ago. This baby is from the sperm he left behind. I had the hospital fertilize my egg with his sperm."

"That's great for you, but that doesn't change the fact that you're a green. The longer you stay in denial, the harder this will be, and the less progress we will achieve today."

"Is this your way of gimmicking me into giving you more money for this? I bet you scam people all the time. I'm a yellow, and I know it."

"In response to your accusation, I'll say the following things…you are here on your own will, I only charge based on donations, and I'm here to help you. I can sense that you're in a lot of pain. You can give me money or you can choose not give me money. The choice is yours. However, I do think it's high time someone told you the truth without dilly dallying around with your time. I'm guessing someone you love told you to come here?"

"Well, yes she planted the idea in my head, but I looked this place up myself." She said with an air of defiant pride.

"You do realize we are the only place of this sort in town, right? Your friend meant for you to find me. And please don't be scared that you have. I'll say this once more before I know I'll sound like a broken record – I'm here to help you."

"Okay. What should I call you then, if you're so destined to help me?"

"My name is Lincoln. They call me Link."

"Okay Link. I'm Abigail. Can you read my aura now?"

"I'd love to." He said as he gazed deeply into and around her at the same time. "You're a healer and a fighter. You've got three different shades of blue, purple, turquoise, and navy blue. Your aura is something special. It's something I haven't seen before."

"That's something anybody could claim to say. Tell me something that makes sense to me. Speak my language. Who am I?"

"That's a great question I wish I could answer. It's too early to know, but you're destined for greatness. The potential I see in you through this crystal ball is unparalleled. You will do things no woman or man, for that matter, has ever done before. You must come back to see me."

Abigail was growing impatient with what seemed like empty words to her and had began tapping her feet. "Well, thank you for your time, but I best get going now."

Link knowingly smiled. "Very well. I wouldn't hold you here against your will."

The two of them walked out of the back room into the main store. It was then that Abigail's mind began to open up to the various herbs, crystals, and incenses she saw all around her in the shop. She then sharply turned to Link.

"Wait, If I'm meant to heal and fight, I wish to do so immediately. I want to be of use to society. I don't want all my pain to have been for nothing. What are some concrete next steps you can recommend to me?" Abigail decided to trust Link with these last few questions. She was still struggling internally with convincing herself that he had her best interest in mind and that this was beyond the two of them.

It was during this mental dilemma that she began to realize how handsome Link was. He reminded her of an older version of her first real boyfriend. His brown locks looked soft and wavy. He was dressed the way she liked her ideal man to be, but she knew she was a little older than him and that he was taken, as indicated by his silver wedding band, so she shook these thoughts as he walked around the store in seemingly deep thought. Now could not be a worse time for her to find a new love interest, let alone one as strange and complex as Link seemed to her.

After strolling around the store, he picked up a quartz crystal and introduced it to her as something that would protect her.

"You'll need this for starters. Keep this on you at all times to ward away the negative energy around you. It'll absorb it all instead of letting it affect you the way it has been. You're far too valuable to be living without one of these on you. Keep it in your purse, your pocket, your house, your car, or wherever else near you. Come back when you need to, and trust me, you'll know when you need to. And one last thing: remember that magic is more about intention and faith than anything else. I wish you the best with getting in tune with your spirit. Come again soon. We'll always be here."

It irked Abigail knowing that he was referring to him and his wife, but on her drive home, she comforted herself in persuading herself that it wasn't jealousy but envy. She didn't want Link, but she wanted a husband the way Link's wife had him. She chalked it up to her own grief becoming too tiresome. Her husband died years ago, and widows weren't supposed to stay widows for long. After all, it was the year 2151.

When Abigail got home, she couldn't help but notice that her spiritual high was nowhere near wearing off. She tried to search for other stores online, but Link was right in saying that The Kiss of Life was the only one in the area. The nearest one aside from it was 35 miles away, but Abigail decided she needed to do this. If she wasn't going to full-heartedly partake in soul-searching, what would she do with her free time? She considered calling up the friend that recommended all of this to her, but decided to wait for a time when she knew more about herself to do so. She wanted to properly express gratitude to her friend in the best way possible, by making her proud. Thus, Abigail decided she'd reach out after becoming more of an expert on her spirit. Why not? She had nothing else going on in her life post-hospital. She reached into her back pocket, where she put the quartz crystal. She tried to remind herself that all she did was visit a store in town, but the whole ordeal was creating an existential crisis within herself. Was she really a green? She had been living her whole life as a yellow. How did she evade the Queen for so long with a mistaken Soul Determination? The harder she clenched the quartz crystal in her fist, the less she decided to dwell on negativities. She began to see the experience in a positive light. It was as if the quartz was melting away all her anxieties. She began to really examine the quartz. She walked to her backyard to look at it properly under sunlight. As she turned it over in her palm, she noticed how beautifully flawed it was. The longer she held it, the stronger she felt a pull from the quartz.

The crystal was about the size of half of Abigail's palm, able to fit snugly in her grasp when she closed her hand over and around it. She decided that it made sense that the more she believed and the stronger her intentions were, the more the quartz would work. She opened her hand again to look at this crystal, which was apparently alive, according to Link. The quartz had a mystical quality and energy to it that Abigail could not describe. It seemed to communicate with her nonverbally. She instinctually ran her fingers up and down the quartz and found that there were countless lines etched in it perfectly parallel to one another. They formed somewhat of a barcode. She noticed that as she ran her fingers up and down this figural barcode, her mind began spinning in ways it had never before. Spiritual powers from centuries of years ago began downloading into her mind in seconds. She started to see who she was in her past life. She was a man – the man who created the universe. She had been God. Not wanting to snap back into reality, she gave into the magic. She reminded herself of what Link had said, that magic was mostly about faith. She began to see how she had died in past lives – suicide. This life had to be different. She needed to do something this time around to change her destiny and the fate of the universe.

The universe and everything we know about it was about to change.

9 IN HER DREAMS

There once was a girl named Astrid, and she had a special power. She could astral-project. She received this power when she wandered through a magical forest and helped a haggard, elderly woman out of a life-threatening situation. It turned out the woman was a witch, and out of gratitude, the witch granted Astrid this power. This power meant that in her sleep, Astrid could make active decisions in her dreams – something most people referred to as lucid dreaming. This proved to be a great use of her time. Most frequently, she would fly through different galaxies and time travel. Her favorite activity was flying back in time to discover that she had a past life, one in which experienced tremendous joy and happiness. When she discovered she was also able to traverse past the three dimensions humans are typically capable of mastering: height, length, and width, she was incredibly excited. She fully understood that time was the fourth dimension, and it left a lot to be explored. She would often fly to see her favorite historical moments unfolding or venture into the future to see what the next day would hold for her. Astrid promised to keep this magic skill a secret, however, so that others would not be jealous and resent her for her special ability.

Another favorite hobby of hers were her journeys to different stars and planets outside of Earth. More often than not, she would visit the Pleiades: an open star cluster that took her around two hours to get to. She was particularly a fan of Pleiadians, because they were all about love, peace, and harmony – something Earth lacked very much of. In fact, Astrid made a lot of friends in the Pleiades, and they would warmly welcome her every time she would astral project there. Since the Pleiadians were far more advanced than Earthlings, Astrid tried to adapt and bring over some of the Pleiadian customs and traditions onto Earth. Astrid would visit the Pleiades on average three or four nights a week in her sleep. How it worked was that Astrid would will herself to sleep every night with a goal in her mind – where she wanted to go, when she wanted to go, and how she wanted to go. Then, her soul would leave her physical body until she could see herself separating from her physical body. There was always a silver chord that attached her soul to her physical body at the belly button, so Astrid would never get lost. Astrid would then fly towards the stars and navigate based off of a mental compass she had in her head. She had memorized the way by now.

The Pleiadians were more advanced than Earthlings in every single way. They lived to be over 700 years old on average as opposed to Earthlings living to be around 80 or 90 if lucky. They healed each other through telepathy and kept each other alive in this way. They also highly treasured women's menstrual blood, using it for gardening, healing wounds, drinking, and marking territory. Female Pleiadians found it a very intimate act to share menstrual blood with their spouses and close male beings by allowing them to drink it, use it in cooking, or to put on their wounds. At first, Astrid shivered with shock at a lot of these customs, but she soon learned to discover the profound wisdom behind it all. Astrid soon learned to accept everything Pleiadian as superior to the ways of Earth.

Astrid also had interactions with other aliens such as the Greys. The Greys were unique in that they were neither male nor female, and they didn't need sustenance to live. In other words, the Pleiadians were far more humanoid that the Greys were. The Greys were hairless as well and had large heads to house their large brains. Their UFOs were far more advanced than any kind of transportation found on Earth, and their military tactics were also far more superior. It seemed most alien beings that Astrid had encountered were able to manipulate the dark matter that is unperceivable by humans despite it being all around us. Aliens could hide within this dark matter to observe humans. We were fascinating to them – mostly how primitive we were. We were like some thought experiment or science project gone wrong. It was embarrassing to be from Earth, Astrid soon learned. While astral projecting, Astrid was in midst of what is called the astral plane, which is the world that souls pass through prior to birth and death. Astrid, however, was able to freely spend time in this plane without restrictions, aside from her soul returning to her physical body upon waking up every morning, but this gave her plenty of time.

As I mentioned earlier, Astrid's favorite astral activity was learning that she had past lives. Though Astrid was a late teenager when she received this power of astral projection, she had lived full lives prior to this one. She had families, jobs, and everything she had always dreamed of. She found that the pursuit of herself was the most fulfilling use of her time. Fortunately, all alien beings she had met in the astral world could also astral project; thus, she was able to bounce ideas off of them and address concerns with them. This helped her deal with the shock of a lot of what she found, especially when it came to exploring the galaxy throughout the space-time continuum. Most significantly, Astrid could converse with angels and God in the astral plane. This is when she met her guardian angel, who became a constant guide to her.

Astrid started to understand little things about herself that she never would have otherwise. For example, Astrid always had a knack for playing the piano and could pick up songs much more quickly than other young adults could. This is because she was a pianist in a past life and would perform sold out recitals and concerts with her skills. Astrid remembers the first time she laid eyes on herself her most recent past life, turns out she had had over 15 past lives, summing up to over a thousand years. Every life was drastically different from the others, and Astrid realized through conversing with God that each of these lives was not a punishment but rather an opportunity to learn a new life lesson. This way, Astrid could keep evolving until she reached higher levels of consciousness and successfully tapped into the divine being of light she always was. After this tremendous realization, Astrid wished that all other humans realized this as well – that they were just temporarily passing through Earth to achieve a goal in this life then move on to a next life somewhere completely different. This profound epiphany hit Astrid like a brick and blossomed within her a great faith for God. She started going to church regularly and was convinced that she loved God more than anyone in the whole congregation and perhaps ever. Astrid knew that she had to channel her faith and knowledge in a productive way, all the while keeping her astral life a secret.

Astrid began loving her astral dream world so much more than her regular, mundane world. She found herself taking every advantage she could to take naps here and there or to sleep in late, thus allowing herself more time in her astral world. She wished she could stay asleep forever. The longer she was asleep, the farther she could travel in this astral world and the more she could discover for herself. She knew that she could be forever in this astral world if she chose to take her life, as this is where people go when they die. Thus, the next morning, Astrid walked down to her father's shed where he kept all his hunting equipment, picked up a rifle from his set, and shot herself in the head. She could now astral travel as much as she wanted to, though having left all of her loved ones in confused agony. She was happier there and had to make the decision out of selfishness.

10 IT'S ALWAYS DARKEST BEFORE THE DAWN

"This is her. She's the Chosen One. Take her away immediately. Alert both the Queen and the Academy," the captain commanded the twelve guards surrounding the room.

"Right away, sir," they all responded with urgency, understanding the gravity of the moment.

The captain nodded and waved the guards off, as they approached the girl the captain held captive for investigation.

"Sir, are you sure we haven't made a mistake today? The Queen will not look favorably upon us if we send her the wrong girl" one of the twelve guards reminded the captain.

"I would bet my life on it. We've witnessed nothing short of a miracle today. Now get to it. We haven't any time to waste," the captain sternly responded.

With these words, the guards grabbed a hold of Esther, the dazed and confused girl standing in the middle of the room in her torn and tattered sundress and escorted her stiffly out of the dark chamber they were in.

Once everyone had left the room, the captain sat down in the nearest chair, buried his face in his hands and began praying to God.

"Father God, I've seen what you can do, and I believe in your love for our people. Please work your magic through Esther, and may she exceed any and all expectations we have of her. The Chosen One is found again, and we aren't going to let her slip away. I pray that she will achieve her full potential under the Academy's guidance. I pray that the Queen will take her under her wings and guide her to the chosen path, for Esther is no doubt the Chosen One. Thank you Father God, for sending us a savior. She will grow to be strong and valiant. The prophets have seen it, and the people believe in it..." The captain continued on until his voice was hoarse and his throat was dry. He then got up and left the chamber himself. He untied his horse from the stable and rode home. It had been quite a long day.

The captain arrived home to his wife asking their children to say grace before dinner.

"Father God, we thank you for this food and drink. We thank you that we may gather together as a family and enjoy this daily bread. Thank you for providing and for looking after us. We live our lives to serve you, our one and only creator. In Jesus' name we pray..." they trailed off as they heard their father's footsteps enter the room.

"And thank you especially for today Lord God, for we have found the Chosen One, our savior today. In your son's holy name we pray - Amen" the captain finished their prayer.

The wife and children all gasped and looked at one another.

"Father, is it true? Have you found her?!"

"Aye, it is true, my sons and daughters. Today was the day. The girl we found was sent immediately to the Academy. The Queen should be getting word any moment now."

The children each scooted to the edge of their chairs and looked up expectantly for more. The captain sensed their excitement but felt far too exhausted to explain the whole day to them. Thus, he began unbuttoning his red peacoat and taking off his hat as he walked towards his bedroom. He plopped himself in bed and fell asleep to the sound of his wife and children chattering about the good news they had just heard. Their land would be saved.

The next day, the captain woke up and rode straight to the Academy – the only place in all the land where magic was allowed. The Academy reached so tall into the sky that no one could see the top from the outside. It was one large oval building that hovered above the ground and was able to float on its own – defying all rules of gravity. Once he approached the Academy gates, the guards at the front each took out their handheld devices and scanned the captain's body up and down.

"Verified. Captain Allan Jackson. Permission Granted," the machine clearly enunciated.

Captain Jackson nodded his head to the guards and handed his horse to them. He then took a whistle out of his red peacoat and blew it with all his might. The sound pierced through the air, and a red dragon descended from the Academy to the Academy gates, the captain hopped onto the dragon, and they both took off to fly to the Academy. The only way to enter it was by dragon. Captain Jackson rode straight to the Queen's lair and found her meditating at her throne while sipping from her silver chalice. She was calm, cool, and collected. She rarely spoke or showed any emotion, but when she saw the captain on this particular day, she smiled from ear to ear.

"You've done it, haven't you, Captain? It's been a long thirty years of your service."

"It has been my honor, my Queen."

"You know the terms of your service. The day you found the savior is the last day you are required to serve."

"My Queen, with all due respect, I would like to continue my service. My life has never been more meaningful. My family, of course, wishes me home, but if you will allow it, I will continue serving you.

"The choice is entirely yours. Who am I to turn away my most loyal confidante?"

"Where is Esther now?" the captain asked, "I would like to see her once more."

"The most I can do for now is let you see through my ball" the Queen responded.

"That will do, my Queen. Anything will do."

The Queen then walked towards a majestic table with gems embedded all over it. On top of the table was a crystal ball – a big, beautiful ball. The Queen waved her hand over the ball, and visions began to appear. The visions showed Esther being born as a baby girl and followed her life in flashes of moments until the present day. The Queen then waved her hand over the ball, and the visions faded.

"But where is she now? How is she handling the Academy?" the captain asked.

"That, I will show you in due time. She is indeed the Chosen One," the Queen responded.

"Let me help train her. I have become not just your captain but also an advanced mage that can assist her in the process of harnessing her powers," the captain requested.

"Don't get too attached to her. She might not make it through the training alive, but we need to train her as hard as we can to stand a chance against the darkness."

"It's always darkest before the dawn," the captain replied knowingly.

"Very well, Allan. Do your best. She's in the Left Wing being sterilized."

"Thank you, my Queen."

Captain Jackson took out his whistle and blew it once again to summon his dragon, which was nearby feeding on fruit trees in the Academy's garden. Captain Jackson mounted his dragon, saluted the Queen, and was off to the Left Wing to find Esther.

"C'mon, Flapper, let's go check on Esther in the Left Wing," the captain whispered to his dragon.

Flapper flew through the Academy with great expertise. She knew it inside and out, seeing as she had lived there all her life and had never left the Academy walls. Just as they neared the Left Wing, the captain saw Esther sitting in a hospital gown with her hair tied back. She had clearly just been sterilized and was waiting further instruction. This was the perfect time to come visit with her, so the captain dismounted his dragon and let her fly free.

"There you are. There's our savior we've waited on for thousands of years. You are the dawn," Captain Jackson beamed.

"I really wish you would all stop with that. I mean I'm honored and all, but this all must be a mistake. How could I be all of the land's Savior? We've been waiting for her for so long; do you realize how disappointing it is for me to realize that I'm that one? I hope the people are ready to be disappointed, because believe me, the bar isn't set very high if it's me we've all been waiting for to save our planet. Just get me out of here. I didn't ask for any of this. I don't want favor from the Queen. I just want to go back to my normal life. I want to go back to my family. I want to-"

The captain raised his hand to quiet her.

"Young lady, do you realize what an honor it is to even be allowed inside the Academy? Look at all this magic around you and understand that you have a place in all of this. Even if you don't believe in yourself, we all believe in you enough to make up for it. Just wait 'til they get you your first dragon, and you set off on your first flight," the captain calmly said, knowing she would eventually come around the more she saw of the Academy and the more she realized her own potential and power.

"You are here to be trained to your full potential. You may not think you are worthy of praise now, but rest assured, in a year or two, you'll be the most powerful magician there ever was. You will surpass not only me, but also the Queen. You will be the Queen of Queens. Kings and Queens of other planets will bow down to your name. You are it. You're our creator in human form. In fact, you are superhuman."

"Just stop it, will you? Can we sit in silence for a few moments? These past two days have been nonstop. Did you send word to my family that I'm here?"

"Oh young lady, soon enough the whole planet will know that you're here once the Queen makes her announcement. Also, may I remind you that you have very little say in the matter. Once you're chosen, you're chosen. You absolutely cannot and will not refuse the call."

Just as the captain finished his thought, a door to the left of them opened, and a guard with a brown pea coat, black tights, and brown boots walked through.

"Esther, let's get you fitted for a training suit and get you started as soon as possible," the guard said.

Esther rolled her eyes, walked past the captain, and through the doors. The captain got up and followed her.

"I will be supervising you from now on. The Queen has allowed me to continue my service for the sole purpose of seeing you through this journey. The training process is arduous. We, as direct servants of the Queen, have all had a taste of the training, but you will need to be plugged into the machine for different reasons than we were. You will be trained with special focus and attention. Now, let's get you hooked up to the machine and start your first simulation."

Esther furrowed her brows as she had heard stories about these machines at the Academy. Everyone had heard of them. They were meant put people through challenges to see how they responded under pressure and in doing so, assess the subjects' character and integrity.

The footsteps of the guard in front of them seemed to move quicker and quicker as they walked down a long corridor. Painted butterflies flew up and down the walls, as the walls displayed art in motion. Magic is what powered them. Esther lost herself in following one particular monarch butterfly, and a smile fell upon her face – one that did not go unnoticed by the captain. He knew that the more Esther saw of the Academy, the less she would take this opportunity for granted.

After a few minutes, the guard, the captain, and Esther reached a large door about five times their size in both height and width. There were two guards standing by at the door who nodded at the three of them and let them in. The big door creaked and opened wide. Esther's eyes widened as she saw what was in the room. There were about a handful of people in sleek, black full body-suits plugged into machines through dozens of tubes connected to the pressure points on their bodies. The guard escorted Esther to a private room to have her fitted for a training suit. Captain Jackson waited by the machines. Esther followed the guard to a private room. As she walked inside the fitting room, the guard gestured that he would be waiting outside for her. Inside the room, stood a woman. No words were spoken as the woman undressed Esther from her hospital gown.

Esther suddenly experienced a bout of fear, knowing that she would soon be plugged into a machine for the first time. She wondered why a place so full of magic relied on machines instead of more magical things like portals, but she supposed these machines relied on magic anyhow, seeing as they didn't rely on electricity or batteries. She had grown up hearing stories about people being plugged into machines and committing suicide the moment they returned from their simulation. Many people couldn't deal with what they saw while hooked onto the machine. They couldn't handle the truth of what the universe had in store. The machines were filled with fake simulations, but these simulations were based off of real occurrences and real circumstances in different places across the universe. Everyone here lived on the planet Juniper and had never travelled to different planets before. Only the Queen had knowledge of different planets through her intergalactic travel privileges as Queen. Thus, she was the one who designed these machines to have realistic simulations. She needed to know who was ready to represent their planet in traveling to other planets with her and eventually taking her place. Needless to say, most people could not survive this process.

The woman in the fitting room took out a piece of black fabric and as soon as the fabric touched Esther's skin, it wrapped around her naked body and covered her from her neck to her ankles. The woman patted Esther on the back.

"Thank you in advance for being the first and only person to complete the simulations alive," the woman couldn't contain herself as she blurted these words out in admiration.

"I haven't even started yet. How can you say such bold words?" Esther asked.

"Because I've seen it. I am one of the Prophets and am gifted with the ability to see people's fates before they embark on their journeys when I suit them up. You are one I don't have to lie to. You will make it. I know you will," the woman said with urgency.

With her new training suit on, Esther was guided out of the room by the guard and towards the captain, who was now standing by an empty machine awaiting them. The machine stood seven feet high, ready to house a human of any size.

Esther stepped up to the silver machine, which was shaped like a pod. Inside the pod was a green gel-like layer that absorbed her body by engulfing it in its juices. Once sunken in, the cold green gel bubbled over Esther's body, immersing her in the machine's essence. The guard hooked up the machine's tubes to Esther's skull, like suctions on her skull.

"Do I get to know anything in advance about what to expect?" Esther nervously asked Captain Jackson.

"That's the whole point, young lady. It's all up to you. Use your creativity and survive. You'll make it far, don't worry. Just remember that you can't die in the simulation," the captain responded.

Esther took a deep breath and sunk into the machine even deeper. Her whole body convulsed as she was mentally transported to a new world. The captain laid his hand on Esther's shoulders and began muttering prayers under his breath. The moment had come for her training to begin.

11 THE THERAPIST I FELL IN LOVE WITH

She floated into the room and smelled like flowers. I immediately knew I was in trouble. My eyes fought the urge to look her up and down. She was so beautiful I could barely breathe. She opened her mouth to say hello, and I nearly fainted – her voice soft like the sea breeze. But the boundaries were all too clear; she was to be my therapist. I knew the rules full well: she couldn't date any of her clients even if I happened to be intriguing to her. Not only that, but she was completely out of my league. I was just a miserable college student hoping to get my life together with the help of professionals. How could she possibly see something in me? I was just one of her dozens of patients. And even if she eventually ever did, what difference would it make? It's not like she would abandon her license just to date me…right? My thoughts spun out of control in the quick first few seconds I laid eyes on her. It was like anxiety at first sight. My heart got caught in my throat, as I registered the fact that she just said hello to me.

"Umm, hi yeah I'm here to see Dr. Frankenson."

"Well then, you're in the right place. Call me Kristen though. I like staying on a first name basis with all my patients."

"Sure, anything, yeah! Hi Kristen. You're beautif - , I mean, I didn't expect you to be so young."

"Thank you, I suppose. I got my hours in earlier on in my career than most, but hey why don't we continue this conversation in the privacy of my office? Please follow me." She said, as she led the way down the carpeted hallway to her corner office. The fact that she had the corner office led me to believe she was either really lucky to have the extra space and extra windows or she earned the right to be in that office.

As I followed her lead into her office, the sun shone in on all the flowers she had in various vases. She must be a gardener. Of course she was a gardener. Why wouldn't she be a gardener? She was more beautiful than all the flowers put together. I shook the jitters out of my head with a physical shaking of my head from side to side. She wasn't beautiful in the sense that she was solely physically attractive, but more in the sense of her general energy and vibes. I could tell she was reserved and thus wise. I've always found that those who have little to say are the ones who have the most important things to say. Focus. Focus. I'm here, because every bad thing that could possibly happen in the past month has happened. Open up and be vulnerable, but be careful, because she's beautiful, I reminded myself. I pinched myself to snap back to reality.

As the session started, I kept everything brief and tried my best to put aside her alluring demeanor to get a good read on her. Was she truly a good fit for me as a therapist or not? I had gone through one too many therapists and had therefore learned to raise my standards higher after disappointingly dropping each one. They were always promising at first, but they would click with me. I needed my therapist to be someone that I could see supporting me time after time and provide the guidance I needed. Since I had interviewed quite a number of therapist, I was able to go on autopilot for a bit as I started asking all the questions I had and bringing up any reservations I had. Of course, I couldn't let Kristen know that I was extremely attracted to her, as that would turn into an incredibly awkward situation that was not her fault. It was up to me to keep my feelings and lust in check.

I tentatively began probing, "What methods do you use to provide therapy to your patients?"

"Good question. I'm quite well-versed in both DBT and CBT. Have you heard of either of those before? Dialectical Behavior Therapy and Cognitive Behavior Therapy?"

I nodded my head with complete understanding, "Yeah I've heard a lot about DBT and CBT."

"Well, I have a few handbooks on those that we can work through together if that suits your style or we can keep these sessions open-ended and discuss anything that comes up for you week by week. What do you hope to be the focus of our time together?"

"I was hoping for specific focus on stress management, grief, and anxiety."

"I see, so we're all across the board here today. Have you had experience with therapy in the past and do you also see a psychiatrist regularly?"

"Yeah I'm on meds and see a psychiatrist monthly."

This back and forth started the session that lasted around an hour. The hour flew by quickly and seemed too good to be true; she seemed like the perfect fit I had been looking for: patient, sympathetic, and understanding.

However, something was still off about the way I thought about her. I felt attracted to her regardless of how much I wanted to snap out of it or how professionally I was able to handle myself. What was I thinking? I don't have time to be adding another problem onto the list of all my other problems. The last thing I needed was to have a crush on a therapist that would've otherwise worked out perfectly for me. I needed a therapist more than I needed a girlfriend right now. After all, in the last month alone, I've experienced more sadness and grief than I have in a long, long time: my dog died, my car broke down, my job was on the line, my student loans were due, and my parents were getting divorced. All of this added to way too much for me to handle at this point. I kind of wanted to give up on life, to be honest. But Kristen came in fast for the save. Maybe I was just vulnerable, but she motivated me to be a better person and to get my act together. She made me want to be desirable. Maybe this wouldn't be so bad after all.

I promised myself I wouldn't fall in love with her, but I knew it would only be a matter of time until I fought myself and broke that promise.

* * *

Now it's been three months since that first day we met, my heart pounds dully and faintly as the ache of grief bleeds lazily out of my soul. I wake up to the comfort of a hospital bed. All I want to do is to call Kristen again. She needs to know why I'm here on this 51/50. I'm on a 72-hour hold at the local EPS – emergency psychiatric services – because I was head over heels in love with her and couldn't get her out of my head. I was hoping this would be an obvious gesture or cry for help to indicate to her how seriously I took our interactions. I felt like a child calling out for a mother, but I couldn't deal with the amount of emotion bubbling up and boiling over inside of me.

I look outside the window, it's still dark out, but there must be a night shift nurse around. I walk outside my room, careful not to wake my snoring roommate. Sure enough, Nurse Bill is in the hallway sitting in his black rolly chair filling out a crossword puzzle.

I approach him endearingly, knowing that the nicer I ask, the better his response is likely to be.

"Hey Nurse Bill, any chance I can use the phone right now to call my mom?" Phone calls in the hospital were meant to be saved for emergencies, but I had to lie to get what I wanted – a chance to call Kristen again. I desperately needed to hear her voice.

Nurse Bill smirks at me, "There's no way you have that much to say to your mom, and I know you better than that at this point. Go ahead and call whoever you want, just don't regret whatever you're gonna say or it'll be on my conscience too."

"Thanks, man." I said urgently, like a meth addict fiending to get high.

IT'S ALWAYS DARKEST BEFORE THE DAWN

I swiftly walk into the conference room where the phone is and shut the door tightly behind me. I run through the last words she said to me inside my head "This happens all the time, dear. It's a term we call transference. Sigmund Freud came up with the concept. You're not in love with me. You're in love with the idea of me. Think about what you actually know about me…very little, I'm certain. Our relationship has been nothing but professional, and you're projecting feelings onto me out of desperation. I say all this with care and fondness. I want you to know that you'll be perfectly fine without me when our sessions are over." I think about how disappointed I was hearing how familiarly these words seemed to come out of her mouth, as if she said this to every other one of her patients. She uncharacteristically sounded like a monotonous machine when she said these words. How could she remain so detached while I was so attached?

I sit there at the conference table, tapping my nervous feet. Finally, I make up my mind not to call her. I go back to my room instead. I shouldn't drag her into this mess. I'm the one who got myself here, and she's right in saying that she was nothing but professional. Why was this all happening? The pain I felt was unparalleled to any other experience in my life, and yet she was feeling nothing on her side. How could I let myself become so hurt? How could I let my guard down?

I manage to fall asleep despite wrestling with these ideas in my head. The next morning I wake up to a nurse coming into my room to take my vitals. As she takes my pulse and blood pressure, I make a mental note to myself that this is my third day of my 72-hour hold. Today, the doctor and I would decide whether I was going home or not. Being at the hospital was certainly a nice getaway, but I had a life to get back to. Finals week was approaching fast in just two weeks. The best part about this hospital stay was that I didn't miss a single class. I didn't have class on Fridays, so I was able to spend Friday and Saturday at the hospital. Today marked Sunday. I knew that I had a therapy appointment lined up for Tuesday with Kristen, just like I did every week. The bright side of all of this is that I could get back to school to see her on Tuesday. A smile formed on my face as I walked down the hospital hallway to have breakfast with everyone else. I had made a few fast friends there and was happy to see them. Just as I was about to take a bite of my cereal, Nurse Bill popped in the room,

"Hey newbie. Phone call for ya. Want to take it?"

"Yeah! Definitely!" I responded with my mouth full.

I got up from the breakfast table and followed Nurse Bill down the hallway to the conference room where the phone was.

"Thanks, Nurse Bill!" I said as I shut the door behind me for privacy.

I saw the "Line 1" button on the phone flashing and got really excited. The only person I told I was at the hospital was Kristen, so it could only be her calling me. I reached for the phone.

"Hello? Alex here" I said

"Hi Alex, this is CAPS calling from Stanford. We wanted to check in with you about your hospital stay. How are you doing? We're here to follow up and provide support for you in the best way possible."

"Thanks! Can I talk to Kristen by chance? Is she in today?" I responded.

"Unfortunately, we can't have you talking to Kristen any more. We feel that your relationship with her has crossed some boundaries and that it is best to assign you a new therapist. We aren't turning you away from our services, we're simply reassigning you to someone who is better suited."

My initial reaction to this was embarrassment. Kristen told them about my feelings, but could I blame her? She was probably obligated to do so and wanted what's best for me. She wanted me to move on, and she was right. I mean, look at me – hospitalized because of a crush. But this was so much more than a crush. This was love. This was potentially marriage. This meant so much more than what anyone else chalked it up to be.

"I don't understand. What went wrong?" I responded, thinking it wise to play dumb.

"We are not allowed to disclose any further information. We hope you can understand. You will now be assigned to Dr. Poon. The hospital will notify us of your discharge, we will see you back on campus when you're ready.

"I understand." I responded.

I hung up the phone and thought to myself "Well, that's that. Kristen spilled the beans, and I'll never be able to see her again."

I walked back to the breakfast room where my new friends were.

"What was that all about? Who called ya?"

"Oh nothing. It was just school wondering when I plan to return."

We sat in silence finishing our breakfasts. I went back to my room to journal and draw until it was time to meet with the doctor about my plans for the future. I strongly requested to return to school after the past three days of recovery. The doctor agreed that I was ready to go and went on a limb to say that I didn't seem to need to be there in the first place, so it was best to open up a hospital bed for someone who truly needed it. I agreed and packed my stuff to get ready to go. After I was discharged, I called an Uber to drive me back to Palo Alto so I could continue pursuing my Literature degree at Stanford.

Monday passed by like a blur. Same old classes, same old routine. When Tuesday came, I picked out a nice outfit to meet Dr. Poon for the first time. I walked to the Vaden Health Center where my CAPS appointment would be located. As I sat there in the waiting room, a scent wafted in that jolted me as I looked up. It was Kristen. I mustered a smile, and she did the same.

"I'm looking for a Sean?" She asked no one in particular.

Sean stood up and followed her into her room. Jealousy consumed me, as I reprimanded myself for confessing my feelings to Kristen. If I hadn't said anything, I would be that Sean seeing her for a one on one session. Another set of footsteps made its way into the waiting room and made direct eye contact with me.

"Alex?"

"Yeah, that's me."

"Follow me this way."

"Thanks."

I was relieved to find that Dr. Poon was a man with gray hair in his late 50s. There would be no problem here.

"What can I do you for today, Alex?" Dr. Poon asked as he seated himself in his black leather armchair and gestured for me to sit on the couch in front of him.

"I fell in love with Kristen and hospitalized myself for being lovesick. That's what's going through my mind today." I couldn't help but be as upfront as possible.

"Well, you certainly don't beat around the bush. I'm familiar with Kristen. All of us counselors work intimately as a team. You might not believe me, but I found myself in Kristen's positions decades ago, when one of my patients professed her love for me. I immediately told my superiors to protect my job security, and I lost her as a patient forevermore. That is most likely how your cards are unfolding as we speak now. I would steer clear of Kristen no matter what, because anything else from you will endanger her job, integrity, and character."

I didn't want to hear these words, but Dr. Poon was right. Who am I to jeopardize Kristen's career? Maybe I can get away with writing her one last letter or note to slip under her door when no one's around. I went home that day satisfied with how my appointment went with Dr. Poon. I was able to be open and honest. This seemed like a fresh start to a hectic chapter of my life. Days became weeks and weeks became years. I finally became a senior and was nearing graduation. On a Tuesday as I walked into Dr. Poon's office, I noticed that the name "Kristen Frankenson" was crossed out from Kristen's door. Ever since that day I met Dr. Poon for the first time, I hadn't seen Kristen. Perhaps she moved on to a new job. I had moved on with my life, and figured that that whole stint was because Kristen caught me at a vulnerable state in my life. That's how I reasoned it out to myself.

After graduation, I got a job overseas in Seoul teaching students English. I always wanted to travel post-graduation, and this job would pay me to do so. As I got my suitcases ready, I called an Uber to take me to the airport. As I got into the car, I noticed flowers dangling from the mirror and a familiar scent all around the car. My driver took off her sunglasses, and her jaw dropped.

"Alex, is that you?"

"Holy hell, KRISTEN?!"

She flashed her pearly whites and seemed happy to see me.

"Where are we off to today?"

"I'm headed to the airport to teach English in Seoul. How have you been?"

"I've been great! I gave up my career at CAPS and am in between jobs right now, just driving Uber to pay the bills until I figure the rest of my life out."

I treasured this information, remember how little she used to share about herself. I suppose that now since she wasn't my therapist, she could say whatever she wanted.

"Come with me." I boldly stated, encouraged by the idea that she left her job and that we were no longer restricted by rules.

She looked into her mirror searchingly to see if I was joking or not.

"I'm serious. Join me. I've loved you all this time."

"So have I, Alex…so have I."

The two of us smiled at each other in silent understanding. What a moment to cherish. This would mark the beginning of the rest of our lives together.

12 BOMBAY OVEN

It was just another Friday. I was on a health leave of absence from Cornell University and back home in the familiar Silicon Valley from the cold Ithaca, New York. I hadn't been feeling well, so I took this leave due to mental health reasons. I had grown accustomed to a quiet, slow life at home as opposed to the fast-paced hustling and bustling college life at Cornell. The two places meant something completely different to me. My main activities every day at home included going to the gym, cooking, cleaning, meditating, journaling, attending church, and other forms of self-care to calm my nerves. At that time, I was in a constant state of either mania or depression and needed to level out my mood with a lifestyle directed towards improving my mental health.

On this particular day, my mom was dropping me off at therapy and going to pick me up after as was the routine for the last few weeks. I wasn't allowed to drive at the time, because my doctor and therapist agreed that I wasn't in a mentally safe space to drive and that allowing me to have car keys could be a fatal mistake. This wasn't a big deal, seeing as my mom was taking time off of work to accompany me on my daily routine and drive me places. I didn't need to leave the house much anyways. Thus, my mom dropped me off at therapy and said she would pick me up in an hour. My session went as it usually did. I was rather stubborn about opening up and being vulnerable, so I mainly bullshitted my way through the session to get the therapist off my back. Going to therapy was my number one commitment and priority, and I had to do it. I would learn to like it later on, but this was during the beginning stages of my journey with mental health.

After my session was over, I walked out of my therapist's office and didn't see my mom anywhere. I texted her and called her, but she didn't respond. This was out of the ordinary, as she was usually reliable and parked right outside my therapist's office. I waited for close to fifteen minutes before I started growing impatient and pacing back and forth. I decided to walk to a nearby Peet's coffee shop to wait for her instead. I knew that I would be able to see her car coming down the road from where I was inside Peet's. As I ordered a quick drink and settled down in the café, I could overhear everyone's abnormally loud conversations, most notably, the ones with the barista who stood a few feet away from my table.

"Hey Josh!" A woman scurried into the café and went right up to the barista. "Did you see what happened next door?!" She asked breathlessly.

"Yeah, I heard something about a car crash?" The barista responded.

"It's a little more than that. More like a building crash! A car ran right into the restaurant next door." The woman urgently explained.

The barista's jaw dropped as he continued, "No way, you're kidding. The Indian restaurant next door? Bombay Oven?"

I registered the conversation and couldn't believe my ears. I knew exactly which restaurant they were talking about. Bombay Oven had been there for as long as I can remember, but how could a car run into a building? The restaurant was separated from the street with a parking lot out front, so the car must've driven all the way across the parking lot and then into the building. It didn't make sense. I tried to process the conversation but eventually shrugged it off and kept my eyes peeled on my phone, still waiting for a response from my mom. Finally, after what seemed like hours later, my phone buzzed. It was my mom. She texted me "I hit building, but I still live." Her broken English was more evident than ever. I couldn't believe it. She was the one that hit the restaurant? It couldn't be.

I had a bad feeling in my gut about it, so I walked outside Peet's and sure enough, my mom was sitting on a curb being questioned by about five or six police officers. Around the scene were two cop cars, two fire trucks, a tow truck, and a large crowd forming. I looked at the damage done. Sure enough, her blue Toyota Camry was completely inside the restaurant past the glass windows and brick wall so far that the only thing that stopped the car from moving any further was the side wall of the restaurant. There were shattered glass shards, broken tables, and demolished chairs everywhere.

I ran over to my mom and asked "What happened? Oh my god. Are you okay?!"

My mom sat in silence, simply shaking her head in disbelief.

From the information I gathered in the next few minutes, I found out everything I needed to know. Fortunately, no one in the restaurant was hurt; my mom was also safe and able to walk away with just a small cut on her finger. This alleviated the situation significantly. It was certainly a close call, since my mom ran over an empty table for a party of 12 that was

IT'S ALWAYS DARKEST BEFORE THE DAWN

running late that day. She could've killed them all if she had done this just a few minutes later. All of their lives would've been in her hands.

There was a mix of shock, relief, and laughter from the crowd. Everyone had their phones out snapping pictures and taking videos. Even the police officers questioning my mom had smiles on their faces and had their own phones out to document the scene. In fact, the following are some pictures of the scene, to give you some perspective on how serious the crash was.

This marked the day that my mom single-handedly took down a restaurant. The restaurant wasn't a popular one, so my mom brushed it off and claimed she was doing them a favor with the insurance money they would get. I couldn't help but shake my head at her.

"Mom this is ridiculous. No one does this kind of stuff except you." I began to lecture her out of concern and frustration.

"This is all your fault. I did this on my way to picking you up. It's your fault you have to go to therapy," she barked as she turned it on me.

I couldn't believe my ears. Was she really going to blame me for this?

As the crowd kept gathering, the tow truck was getting positioned to tow the car out, and my mom and I just sat there. I was suffering from severe secondhand embarrassment, but she seemed unfazed by the whole ordeal and just sat there in a calm silence, as if this whole fiasco was premeditated.

After about ten to fifteen minutes, my aunt and uncle showed up to the scene to help out. I assume my mom called them for moral support. I was glad to see them, as their presence diffused the tension between my mom and myself. After giving both of us hugs, my uncle immediately picked up the phone and started talking to the insurance company about options, while my aunt walked around the scene taking pictures at all angles. Meanwhile, the tow truck began pulling my mom's Camry out of the restaurant.

It really was a miracle that no one was hurt and allowed the situation to be more comical than it was serious. After an hour, everything started to resolve itself, and the police began leaving one by one. The crowd also began to disperse as the sun began to set, making it dark out. After my mom collected her possessions from the Camry, my aunt and uncle drove both my mom and me home.

After going home and unwinding from the day, I logged onto my computer and the first thing I saw was a bunch of notifications and pictures on my newsfeed. Pictures of my mom's car inside Bombay Oven were going viral; it was a small world in my hometown of Cupertino. News travelled fast, especially via social media.

Imagine my surprise when a few days later, my mom suggested we all go eat at the restaurant as a family. Apparently, the half that wasn't demolished was still in operation and seating guests for lunch and dinner. Thus, we decided to make it a family affair and invited all the family in the area. This was about a party of ten of us. We got to the restaurant, and sure enough, half of it was completely destroyed and roped off, while the other half was fully functioning. Naturally, the waiter that was serving us was the one who was there the day of the car crash. I was surprised at how unfazed my mom was by all of this. I know I personally wouldn't have had the nerve to walk into a restaurant that I single-handedly destroyed. It was one of the most awkward dinners I had ever had, as the waiter took our orders and served us the rest of the night while we sat facing amidst the ruins of the restaurant.

IT'S ALWAYS DARKEST BEFORE THE DAWN

It's been about around 5 years now since the Bombay Oven incident, and now Bombay Oven is completely replaced by a Vitamin Shoppe and a Blaze Pizza. The whole area looks a lot more urban and modern. My mom continues to claim to this day that Bombay Oven should thank her, since it was a restaurant that needed an excuse to disappear. We were just grateful no real harm was done, so we could genuinely laugh about it. It has now become a running joke in our family to remind my mom to not run into any restaurants on her way anywhere in the car. To this day, my mom still blames me for this accident. Sometimes, I wonder if she did all of this for the attention or to give me a wakeup call. It's difficult to unintentionally drive into a restaurant, so no one was ever convinced when she explained what went through her head as she drove into the restaurant "accidentally." It's hard to get into the mind of my mom, so I guess we'll really never know the truth. What surprises me most is how little trouble she got into and the minimal negative consequences and repercussions of the crash. She didn't even get a ticket or anything. The police asked her a few simple questions, laughed it off, and went on their way. Afterwards, she wasn't contacted about it whatsoever, whether to pay for any of any the damages or own up to what she did. I guess you could call it the perfect crime.

Additional Poems

SAYING GOODBYE

Saying goodbye is always hard,
Especially when you've finally learned to let down your guard.
The risk of making friends
Is never being able to see them again.
Everything was worth the risk,
Even if the encounters were brisk.

Emotions running high here and there,
But there's nothing but professionalism in the air.
We've built up strong walls to keep boundaries straight,
It's funny that it's only in these settings, we're free of hate.

Walking through life alongside each other,
Will always make it all the better.
Saying goodbye seems nothing short of cruel.
Who's the one who came up with the rules?
Human connection is human connection.
However you spin it.

The pain and grief of losing those that have helped me grow the most,
Sure makes me feel like an empty soul and ghost.
What will I do without safety, love, and support?
It's certainly more than I get from my typical social cohorts.
I need a purpose,
And to allow my pains to surface.

There's still a lot I don't know,
But it looks like we're reaching the end of the show.
It's time to part ways,
And I have to try my best to not let my stability sway.
It's just a goodbye after all, isn't it?

I sure will miss you,
Even though I'm really not supposed to.
But some things just stick to me like glue,

CORDY JIANG

Like these memories that I'm trying not to let turn me blue.
I'll always have a special place for you.
Deep within my soul in a place that I know is true.

You know what the rest of them say.
"Don't cry because it's over.
Smile because it happened."
So, here's to me faking a smile.

IT'S ALWAYS DARKEST BEFORE THE DAWN

WE ALL HAVE OUR STRUGGLES

We all have our struggles,
And sometimes it's much more than we can juggle.
But if we don't stay strong and persist,
We will no longer know or want to exist.
Waking up every morning thinking something is wrong,
Is not the way to feel or belong.

Having more faith in ourselves than our demons,
Will help lead us back to dreaming.
Remember the dreams we used to have as kids?
When we didn't have to worry about all this?
Life only changes when you allow it to,
Think outside the box, rather than being trapped in your own zoo.
We're more than just hard-wired animals.
We don't have to suffer from life being mechanical.

We can take initiative and steer our own lives.
We can get out of all the strife.
We can muster up the strength to rise.
We can soar into those blue skies.

Whatever your problem is,
Think about when you were a kid -
When the world hadn't tainted you yet,
Before you started to forget
To hold onto what made you you,
And gave into the mind that is that zoo.
So it is to these negative thoughts you need to unglue.
Why don't you show the world colors other than blue?

If you think you're the only one suffering,
Boy, do you have it wrong.
We all march to a different beat,
And sing along to a different song.
But at the end of the day,

CORDY JIANG

We are all molded of the same clay.

So don't you forget others suffer just the same,
And that we are all playing this twisted game.
Let me tell you, only the strong ones survive,
So it's time to start acting alive
Instead of stalling in overdrive.

A SEA OF GRIEF

I once drowned in a sea of grief.
I was able to surface for air once I admitted the truth,
That I was unable, unwilling, and uncompromising.
I no longer wanted to live without you around.
I now find myself in these similar, familiar situations.
Where you aren't always there, and I always am.
I try to wait for a glimpse of the ghost of you,
But instead, I remember how I drowned in that sea of grief.

Theoretically, I'm no longer alive.
I remain on this earth to think of you but to never have you.
You're in a distant world with distant people.
We can no longer connect the way we used to.
Everything has changed now,
And I can sense all the difference.

I remember pedaling and treading,
Fighting the weight of the water on me.
But it was all to no avail.
I let myself drown,
That's the real truth, and I know it.
But I still let myself drown.
What else would I do without you?

I felt stripped of my hope, joy, and optimism.
Suddenly, I was finding myself in places I had been before.
Familiar places hidden in the darkness,
In the shades of the trees that towered so highly.
I knew not but to grieve over the loss of you.
Feeling the pangs of emptiness and longing wash over me.

I kept pushing for positivity,
A glimpse of a truth I wanted to believe,
But at the end of the day,
That same sea of grief washed over the shores,
Only allowing me to be drawn in by the waves.

CORDY JIANG

The higher the moon rose,
The closer I was to my demise.

May nobody experience the pain I have,
And may nobody grieve over me either.
Just be thankful
Of the time that we have had together
No matter how long or short.

SELF-PERCEPTION

Who can say they don't look in a mirror?
It's a necessary act for one to be clearer,
About one's identity and one's projection,
Perfecting oneself for the sake of protection.
We see ourselves as we do,
But no one person holds that very same view.

To understand oneself fully is to lose sight of life's purpose,
The process of life will never leave one voiceless.
We cannot get lost in the trap of introspection,
When the true key is to see one's own reflection.

Do we see what others see when they look at us?
Or are we all just strangers sitting side by side on a bus?
Does being vulnerable and fragile lead to trust?
Or should we all try to be fair and just?

Perception is a tricky beast,
It can make us all turn our heads East
As the sun rises to shed light on our masks
While under deception, we bask –
Not one of us showing our true selves,
Out of fear of being as boring as bookshelves.

So who is it that does the real perceiving?
Is it the One we all believe in?
Does God hold all the answers and truths?
While only clueing us in out of ruth?

I see myself as a well-kept secret.
I hide it all, so they don't see it.
I can barely see it myself,
Without scattered help.

CORDY JIANG

WRITING IS LIKE WALKING

Writing is all about taking life in stride,
Writing teaches you that in life there's nothing to hide.
Even though we learn to walk before we learn to write,
Words will forever and ever be by our side.
You can learn to write from reading,
Or you can learn to write from breathing.
Some find beauty in other people's words,
While others find beauty from walking until it hurts.

We don't always need to walk in the right direction
To know that life is a continuous progression.
We can put socks on our feet and shoes on our socks,
But life's paths will always be covered with rocks.

Some people walk with ease,
Some people walk with disease.
When it comes down to it,
It's about making it all fit:
Joy, harmony, love, and wholeness,
These are all the keys to eternal bliss.
So when you take your next step,
Remember to add that extra pep.

Crawling becomes walking,
Walking becomes running,
And running becomes flying.
Don't let yourself stop just because you think you're dying.
Take a step back to take two steps forward,
And while doing so, be sure to stay true to your world.

THEY JUST DON'T GET IT

they just don't get it.
they just wait 'til everyone's upset and
leave a mess for everyone to clean up
when they're the ones that need to sober up what's in their cup.

they say the squeaky wheel gets the grease,
so i guess only those wheels feel the release.
release from turmoil, release from pain,
while everyone else is left to strain in vain.

so how do we make our problems known?
when they're the ones seated on the throne.
why don't they pick on someone their own size,
and let the rest of us keep our eyes on the prize?

but at the end of the day,
let's not let our thoughts run astray,
or wait for the results to delay.
all we need to say
is that they just don't get it,
nor will they ever come to regret it.

CORDY JIANG

LISTENING

I can listen to myself or I can listen to my friends,
It is upon them that virtually all my guidance depends.
They seem to be psychic and know what happens in the end.
But it's only a matter of time before on my own, I will fend.

They can tell me what I should say and what I should do,
But at the end of the day, to my own self I will be true.
We all run into life's obstacles and hurdles,
But we should never let anything make our blood curdle.
When you reach that point of seemingly no return,
That's when you make it someone else's turn –
Someone to guide you and lead you,
Someone that can handle being in your circle of few.

I will have you know,
That whether you listen or not will visibly show.
As you begin to let life's flow
Be interrupted blow after blow.
But facing and fighting hardship will only help you grow.

You are the company you keep,
So make sure you don't lose a wink of sleep,
Letting people get to you who are nothing but creeps.
Into your life, they will try to seep.
Until they get the satisfaction of seeing you weep.

Be careful where you tread and be sure to tread lightly,
For if you make all the right choices, you will start to shine brightly.
It's always darkest before the dawn,
And you learn to turn from a little duckling into a swan.
Listen to those who love, and avoid those others who only shove,
For they will try to turn you every which way,
And pretend to be close to you only to betray.

Hate is like a disease that festers in your heart,

IT'S ALWAYS DARKEST BEFORE THE DAWN

And soon you will want someone to love for a fresh start,
So listen to others but don't let yourself be consumed,
Because hate will stand in the way and fill you with gloom,
But love will help you learn how to bloom.
From the time you leave your mother's womb to the time you enter your tomb,
Always keep an ear out for who listens to whom.

CORDY JIANG

SURFACE FOR AIR

I can't breathe when I look at you.
It's like you've filled my lungs with thick, viscous glue.
Most people can't breathe without you,
But I can't even breathe around you.
Tell me how that's fair.
Tell me not to despair.
Tell me I can't surface for air.

You disable me…I'm afraid to be
There, where you are
Your eyes just like stars.
Your hands holding my heart.
And me, grasping for air.
Your stare keeping me there.

When I look at you,
You all but look away.
You know that there's no way
That I'm there to stay.
I can only be there on display,
While my mind escapes far, far away,
As I stand there like weak prey.

How I wish I could piece my thoughts together,
How I wish to chat about the weather,
and how I wish my heart weren't chained to your tether.
How is it I hang onto your every word when we're together,
While you bounce around light as a feather?

I always walk away in great dismay,
Knowing that I've ruined my own day,
Not being able to say what I needed to say
And having failed in a dark, unforgiving way.

So, I tell myself life goes on,

IT'S ALWAYS DARKEST BEFORE THE DAWN

But we all know the true tune of the swan song.
I've wasted a chance I simply could not prolong,
While I try to justify that I did all I could to stay strong.
Life truly cannot and will not move on,
The moment you say you're gone,
For that's when I lay awake for many dawns
Knowing that in your eyes,
I will always be but just a little pawn.

THE IN-BETWEEN

The quiet of the in-between
Is so deafening that I could scream.
Silence has never been so loud,
As raindrops fall from my clouds.
I simply hide myself beneath the shrouds,
Until out go all the crowds.

I look at myself and wonder what happened,
My reflection changes every time I sadden or madden.
I take on a new look, a new identity,
But all I see in myself is a familiar enmity.
Do I hate who I am?
Why is that so hard for others to understand?
How do I love myself?
When no one is there to help?

I can't stand to be alone,
I wish I had a custom-made clone.
Someone to follow me around like a drone.
Someone that I could perhaps call home,
Even when all my sins are known.

Alas, I remember God is there for me,
He is as faithful as there ever can be.
So why would I disagree
That I am supposed to be satisfied with just me?
I wonder if God remembers I cannot see the true me
And my reflection only shows me who I'm supposed to be,
Despite my desperate cries to be set free
And rewrite my whole autobiography.

So why am I torn?
And why am I my own thorn?
Maybe I am instead listening to the one with horns,
Because we all know how loudly the devil can scorn.

IT'S ALWAYS DARKEST BEFORE THE DAWN

If only I could replace my mind with positivity instead,
Maybe then I wouldn't be filled with this perpetual dread.
Maybe then my blood wouldn't run red,
And maybe then, I could calmly lay my head on my bed.

Every night is a struggle,
As I treat life like a juggle.
And end up going to sleep befuddled.

CORDY JIANG

EMPTY

I am feeling awfully empty inside,
In a place where no one is on my side.
It is like everyone has left me high and dry.
It is a feeling I cannot deny.
So why does it not help when I cry?
And when I reach out,
All they do is pry.

Restricting myself from simple pleasures,
Has become easier and easier,
As I reach new levels of understanding.
I am like wood that needs sanding.
As I slowly learn there is no perfect landing.

Mentor after mentor disappoint me,
As some fellowship do not come for free.
Sometimes when people try to help you,
They end up making you feel more blue.
And there is some pain that people cannot just undo.
So it is up to me to get a clue,
As I do everything but misconstrue.
I will do me and you will do you.

The dark emptiness seizes me even as I distract,
When I am in public, I forget how to react.
People are talking to me front and back,
And I realize my vision goes black.
As I start to retract.

I try to rearrange my activities to fill time,
But I realized I am going through life like a mime.
Have nothing to say but a whole lot in my mind.
When I think about my day,
I just want to press rewind.
I could have done this and that,

IT'S ALWAYS DARKEST BEFORE THE DAWN

But my mind is on overdrive.

I find myself tracing back to my roots for hints,
To find out when, where and why I have these stints.
But when I am looking at my past, I always wince,
Because I always look deeper than a quick glimpse.
So join me on my journey as I delve in to the present,
Because we are not even close to getting into heaven

CORDY JIANG

RENEW

In order to find myself,
I had to pull myself away from you.
Suddenly all the clouds turned from white to blue.
It is not the same without my muse.
It seems that I am missing all of life's clues.
I have withdrawn from my social groups,
As I seek after that one renew.

My parents seem to be the source
That pardons me from my guilt and remorse.
They are aware of my sins past to present,
And have nudged me toward my moral ascent.
I dread the future, as it is so uncertain,
I wish I could just push past these thwarting curtains
That restrict me to my current hurting.

I wish to break free and push through,
As I once did from my mother's womb.
I seek after a comfort that I only know now as paternal,
Something that is present everyday and even eternal.
A soul that knows mine at the end of everyday,
And feels the pains and joys of my life's decay.
Someone who can meet me in the middle,
Of all my faults and hurdles.

What is it that I really want?
Someone who is unapologetically blunt?
Or one who knows how to avoid any stunt.
I know I could use someone to lean on like a crutch,
Someone whose care and advice would be clutch.
And hopefully someone who is not addicted to snuff.

I am not as specific as some may get,
I just cast out a big, wide net.
Whatever creatures cling on will be considered,

IT'S ALWAYS DARKEST BEFORE THE DAWN

Any shape and size of a sea critter.
I would like to find one that not only catches my eye,
But also realigns me when my life goes awry.
One that reassures me of my skills,
And brings out life's thrills.

We all go through peaks and valleys,
But hopefully my life is right down your alley.

CORDY JIANG

THESE FOUR WALLS

I sleep when I am awake and am awake when I sleep.
The four walls that enclose me
Make sure that nobody knows me
They hide who I am and necessitate privacy.
The deciding factor is if you would shine light on me.
For I would like to experience being happy and free.

These four walls have opinions and thoughts of their own,
Stifling the mentalities that I have learned to call home.
I often wonder if people can see right through me like I see right through them.
To them I may be nothing, but I sincerely consider everyone else a gem.
Despite this heightened view of everyone,
I know that you would still be the most fun.

If I do not play favorites then I do not survive,
I hope you do not find my communication too contrived.
You are the one that can pull me through,
All of this emotional debris and residue.
Please do not get my intentions misconstrued.

With all these people in the way,
It makes it hard for me to come out and play.
I hope that you can call my bluff,
Because life without you is nothing but rough.
I see the redness in your eyes and the lines on your face,
Why can you not see all you need is my embrace.
I can save you from your problems,
Or at least help you solve them.
I want to bear your burdens,
I want to see you jump through all those hurdles.
I can give you a lift to jump over,
And I can be your lucky charm like a four-leaf clover.

These four walls hide me from you and you from me,

IT'S ALWAYS DARKEST BEFORE THE DAWN

But the intangible agreement of our mutual love,
Can provide us peace like a soft, white dove.
We can be connected through our love of the one up above.

Your morals, values and ethics,
Are right in line with my personal politics.
So show me more of you,
As I seek the Lord through you.
This love can never be subdued.

CORDY JIANG

BUSY BUMBLE BEE

Do I have to be mean to make you get it?
Do I have to be a jerk to make you see?
You're being pushed around like their busy bumble bee.
Everything you do eases their troubles,
And trust me, they want to do more than just cuddle.
The pains you experience and the hurdles you cross,
Are nothing to them because they are your boss.

Forever more shall you be in servitude,
And from them you will never receive gratitude.
If you listen to and heed my words,
You will discover how to avoid being hurt.
I have years of experience on my hands,
And every day of those years went unplanned.
When you have a solid plan and foundation,
No strong wind can change your sails.
Even when you think you can do nothing but fail.

It is about seeking help before it is too late.
To plan prevention before the horse is let out of the gate.
The bee would never sting the horse though,
Even if it were all for show.
Some animals do not have a bad bone in them,
Until they realize that not everyone is their kin.
And that their kin does not guarantee no sin.

In a mix of words and sentiments,
I hope to pass along
the counseling and advice that I have built upon.
Three to four years of tumultuous recovery,
Have helped me to stop and look at the shrubbery.

It takes a lot of hard work to undo,
All the bondages that cling to you like glue.
The world seems satisfactory in the perspective in which you see it,

IT'S ALWAYS DARKEST BEFORE THE DAWN

Until you meet someone who cares enough about you
To unscrew your life and lay it all on the line.
To analyze each interaction since the beginning of time.

Some of the greatest people that have influenced me have been my therapists.
There's something about understanding a situation that makes healing efficient.
The hesitation of paying someone to be your best friend subsides,
When you realize they are some of the few people that will remain on your side.

CORDY JIANG

PHASES OF ANGER

There are so many different phases of anger,
It's like an onion being peeled in layers.
An initial shock and realization occurs,
When denial and acceptance are deferred.
Anger subsides into forgiveness,
But neither party is ever able to fade to abyss.
Events are forgiven and not forgotten,
And what was once ripe is now rotten.

At first, there is a motivation to almost kill,
But then you realize this is just a hill.
A hill of emotions and turmoil,
A hill with hard to tread soil.
Then you tap into one of your chakras,
And realize that you just need to give it up to God.
If he wrote the beginning, he will certainly write the end.
And if you sin in any way, do not expect him to bend.

Everyone is different and I am grateful for that,
If we were all the same then Hogwarts wouldn't need a sorting hat.
We fish around for reasons why to believe,
When in reality, we need to stop wearing our hearts on our sleeves.
When I refer to we, I refer to a very select few,
That seems to find solace in repenting at the pews.
Religion represents humility,
A recognition that life is not just you and me.
Someone else is greater, better and stronger.
All the more to worship him longer.
He is not a sinful man trying to rally support.
He is a spirit that is with us in all our cohorts.

How does me trying to evangelize you relate to anger?
Well, at least it places me in the position of a stranger.
But I hope to be much more,
As I long for you to soar.

IT'S ALWAYS DARKEST BEFORE THE DAWN

I wish for you to soar me with me as free as can be,
Above the blue skies and dark seas.
We can find happiness altogether,
Leaning on one another.
As we learn to forgive our sisters and brothers.
And realize that anger is just a twisted form of love,
And that we must experience faith, hope and joy,
Even if that means you no longer being someone's toy.

CORDY JIANG

CUPID'S ARROW

Cupid's arrow must be coated in venom,
Because my thoughts of you are like poison.
They cover me every day like denim
And blast my ear off with strange noises
Until I can't even see what the point is.

They say there are plenty of fish in the sea,
But it looks like slim pickings when it comes to you and me.
All I want is that one shot to win your love,
Because you and I could fit like a glove.
But it all comes down to the One that's above.
And I already know it would take more than a shove.

I feel frantic when I don't find you there,
It's like a desperate, dying lack of air,
When you aren't there to share
Everything that I hold dear
From which stems my undivided care.

ANY MINUTE NOW

Any minute now,
The press will tear me down.
I'm walking every which way,
Just trying to stay away
Before they lock me up like a stray.

The mental hospitals and halfway houses,
Kept me silent and docile like church mouses.
Every time I felt like expressing my opinion,
The doctors, shrinks, and nurses treated me like a minion.
And the medications had me cringing.

When I have my freedom back,
I get back on the right track,
And the keyboard goes click clack,
As I write the one and only soundtrack.

CORDY JIANG

EVERY LITTLE BIT

Every little bit counts, no matter what they say
Whether it's in or out, to or from, up or down, around and about
Every word, penny, thought, worry, frustration
All of this comes together in a combination
A combination that makes the world go round
Recycling its own energy over and over

Whether it's psychic energy, physical energy or another
Everything with everyone happens how it should
It fits into itself like a piece of a giant puzzle
And can cramp you down like any other muzzle

There are certain paths in life you shouldn't take,
But how many paths are we given if people don't make mistakes,
We are creatures of habit, see an opportunity and just wanna grab it
Not knowing the consequences of the lack of patience, the almighty virtue

Every word, thought and action leads to a certain behavior,
With that, no one can be called our Savior
Everyone's got their own set of everything,
Which makes us give credit to nothing

Everything we need is all around us,
It's compassion and empathy we need,
A necessary deed to help the nation in need,
A deed needed to be felt and done by absolutely everyone.

IT'S ALWAYS DARKEST BEFORE THE DAWN

BEING STILL WITH THE SILENCE

Being still with the silence
Means blending in with the crew,
Knowing when and where your cue is.
The luck of the draw ain't so hot all the time,
But that's when you make it out of what it isn't
By being still with the silence.

Not all of us have what it takes
To make a happy future and succeed,
It's about patience, hard work, and sacrifice
Something you won't want to do twice.
Something that calls for every last advice
Being still with the silence

Sometimes it isn't stop or go
It's about letting go of all control
And falling into the hands of the plan
To lose the need to hurry up and cram
By being still with the silence.

At peace with it all,
There's only a short length to fall
Cradled in the snug fit of life,
Every phase can just as well cut like a knife.
It all depends on who and what you've done
To deserve what's considered fun
Life can throw curveballs
Or flow down like waterfalls.

CORDY JIANG

OH THE POSSIBILITIES

The possibilities are endless, they always say.
But where are the easy ones, I've looked all day.
Every dream is another mile, another marathon.
Leaving me with no cloud to fall back upon

You could search all day for the chances you've got,
But you'll find the ones you want put you on the spot.
They make you risk everything you have for one shot,
And clear the way so you don't get caught.

We exclaim at the sight of a dream, exalt
When the journey there becomes nothing but our fault
We learn the hard way that everything comes at a cost.
And if you don't get there first, it'll all be lost.

You've got to work hard and get your face in dirt, you see
For all we know, misery loves company.
We'll all toil in it together then,
All trying to make it in the same vision

After you give it a lot of hard work and time,
You'll have what it takes to make it "mine"
But it's the diligence and patience that pass the test,
And allows the great ones to finally get some rest
While others are weeded out before becoming the best.

THE LONESOME BABY

A lonesome baby girl stands before
A wooden house with crooked construction.
She stands with rags put together by a single button.
The dull earrings on her ears tell the tale
Of her life of destruction.

She longs for a family close to her,
She finds no source of education
Other than her own imagination.
She begins to forge a life filled with
Solitude and independence.

She gazes into the camera's eyes
With speculation and hesitation.
She knows not what her purpose is in this life yet,
But she doesn't realize life holds more for her than
The failures around her.

Failures are made into successes.
Her hardships will create new beginnings,
She will soar into her life with a sense
Of modesty, courage, and appreciation.

CORDY JIANG

MAKING CHANGE

To make change, you gotta mean it.
You need to inspire a fire within you.
Change is waiting to be made,
Change after change can occur
Upon your call.

Everything's ready, all systems go.
The one person lagging is you.
Make that change.
Go see it happen before your eyes.

Change is something that happens when you ask for it.
You need to instill pride in someone
To embarrass them into change.
That's the ultimate length to go.
Someone who'll do that for you is a keeper.

Change can be in the shape of anything,
But once it comes, it's there to stay
And you get to marinate in its difference.
And when you do,
You'll know victory is rooted in hard work and turmoil.

AGAINST THE WIND

Every morning you wake up and crack open a window,
The fresh air beckons as you test the air with a finger.
Which way is the wind blowing today?
And how can I blow against it.

Wind's so strong, it blows to and fro.
Soon enough, everything's blowing in the same direction.
When all I wanna do is scream stop
Because I'm running right up against it

They call it leading by example,
I call it knowledge of the fittest.
I earned the wisdom I have,
Through dungeons and pits of doom.

I've beat the test of time,
I'm still here standing,
Ready to spew my story out
To the world's ear,
Awaiting my next big thrill.

CORDY JIANG

DISCOVERED

To be discovered is a beautiful thing.
You learn to trust and let go of inhibitions.
You learn that you may embrace life
And life will embrace you back
An embrace filled with warmth, passion and fortitude.

To be found doing what you love most,
Is a penetrating and eternal pathway;
Honored by those around you who love you,
And leads you to pure happiness.

There aren't many challenges that can
Get in the way of you and your destined path
Once you've conquered everything leading to it.
When you've started forging a path,
You've already been discovered.

Discovery saves souls and lives.
It combines the strengths of your weaknesses
Into a great sum of your future.

IN THE CALM

Flustered and sweating all over,
I can't seem to remember what you
Were trying to say in the calm.
We enter such different realms,
I can't pinpoint what emotion you say you mean.

The song can only capture so much
But I know you can feel what I feel.
I wear it on my sleeve,
While you wear it inside.

As you wear it inside,
You hide a part of yourself from me.
The part which eludes me most
Allures me most.

We banter and bicker back and forth,
We haggle and straddle back and forth,
We love back and forth.

CORDY JIANG

WANNA

Do you wanna join me on the dancefloor?
I've never taken any lessons but I sure can lead.
You dance two steps and I'll dance four,
I'll show you how to be held and you show me your smile.

I'll clap for you as you dance and laugh,
You'll dance and laugh like there's no morning.
We'll be partners on the dancefloor.
Dancing up a happy storm.

One of us leads and one of us follows,
But we can switch off mid-song no problem.
Whatever floats your boat, I follow anyways.
Dancing is teamwork,
It's a give and take, a push and pull.

How many partners have you danced with before,
Because you seem to be giving a little too much.
Let me take your hand and twirl you around,
It's your turn to be pampered and shown off

Just please don't fall in love.

COME AS YOU ARE

Come as you are,
I don't need a thing more.
I want you
For all your worth
And however you are,
At this very moment.

You said you'd remember me forever.
And then I cried.
I knew we'd grow apart;
I never thought it'd be this fast though.

If you've kept true to your word,
You'd have a photographic memory of our saga.
You used to say the best part about memories,
Is that we can keep them forever.

We were like oil and water,
Polar opposites yet perfectly beautiful when mixed.
You were the jalapeno pepper to my guacamole;
The one who got me through life with a little spice.
The one that fed me a little taste of death.

THE END

ABOUT THE AUTHOR

Cordy (Cordelia) Jiang is a young and budding author who studied Literature - specifically Creative Writing - at UCSC. She grew up in Cupertino, California in the Silicon Valley, where her family resides today. After a busy life in high school serving as ASB President, participating in multiple sports, and playing in the marching band, she went on to study Hospitality Administration at Cornell University. However, shortly afterwards, she took a health leave of absence during which time she was hospitalized on and off for five years. It is from these experiences struggling with mental health and interacting with other patients that she draws most of her inspiration from for her writing. Her battle with mental health has been deeply personal. She hopes that through her writing, she can give a voice to some of these disturbing but necessary topics and to shine a light on what people grapple with on a daily basis.

Made in the USA
Columbia, SC
03 May 2024